The Man

Phoebe held her hands c ... ove *The Book of Shadows*. She recit... incantation in a low, sing-song voice.

In the next moment, the air at the far end of the attic began to shimmer. That's more like it, Phoebe thought. Soon she'd have her answers.

The specter seemed to explode into view. Phoebe couldn't tell if it was male or female, which somehow made the wolflike Halloween mask that it wore all the spookier.

Of course, the truly spooky thing was the enormous knife in the ghost's right hand. Slowly, menacingly, the ghost approached Phoebe.

"Keep out," it told her in an inhuman voice that made Phoebe's flesh crawl. "Keep out. Keep away."

"Who are you?" Phoebe asked, her voice shaking. Then she realized—she was alone in the attic with the perpetrator of the Halloween murders!

Phoebe shrieked as the ghost took another menacing step toward her, lifted the knife, and brought the blade down toward her chest.

Charmed™

The Power of Three
A novelization by Eliza Willard

Kiss of Darkness
By Brandon Alexander

The Crimson Spell
By F. Goldsborough

Whispers from the Past
By Rosalind Noonan

Voodoo Moon
By Wendy Corsi Staub

Haunted by Desire
By Cameron Dokey

Pocket Pulse
Published by Pocket Books

HAUNTED BY DESIRE

An original novel by Cameron Dokey
Based on the hit TV series
created by Constance M. Burge

A Parachute Press Book

POCKET PULSE
New York London Toronto Sydney Singapore

This book is a work of fiction. Names, characters, places and incidents are products of the author's imagination or are used fictitiously. Any resemblance to actual events or locales or persons, living or dead, is entirely coincidental.

An *Original* Publication of POCKET BOOKS

POCKET PULSE published by
Pocket Books, a division of Simon & Schuster, Inc.
1230 Avenue of the Americas, New York, NY 10020

ISBN: 0-671-04167-3

First Pocket Pulse printing October 2000

10 9 8 7 6 5 4 3 2 1

POCKET PULSE and colophon are trademarks of Simon & Schuster, Inc.

Printed in the U.S.A.

HAUNTED BY DESIRE

CHAPTER 1

He loves me. He loves me not. He loves me. He loves me not. He loves me—"

"Prue, what on earth are you doing?"

Prue Halliwell gave a start at the sound of her younger sister Piper's voice. She had been scattering daisy petals all over the living room floor.

Quickly, Prue grabbed the vase that held the remains of the bouquet she'd been picking apart. She stood up, as if she were about to take the flowers into the kitchen and put them out of their misery in the more usual fashion.

"Piper," she complained, hoping a quick offensive maneuver would throw her sister off the track, "now look what you made me do!"

Piper Halliwell laughed, her high heels clicking against the hardwood floor of the hall. She was dressed to go out in a slim sheath of dark blue silk. She fastened a pair of sparkling earrings to her ears as she moved.

The Halliwells had a Monday evening dinner date, a togetherness event for some sisterly quality time. The only one missing was the youngest Halliwell, Phoebe. Interesting that this whole idea had been hers to begin with.

"Oh, no," Piper said, doing her best to fix Prue with a steely-eyed stare and failing miserably. "I didn't make you do anything. And don't think you can distract me, either. I saw you behaving in a totally un-Prue-like manner. You're busted. Now spill the beans. What were you doing to those poor flowers?"

In spite of her annoyance at being caught, Prue fought back a smile. Watching Piper try to act tough was like watching a bunny rabbit bare its teeth. Still, Piper had a point. Prue's atypical behavior probably did warrant some sort of explanation.

The only problem was, she didn't have the faintest idea what explanation to offer.

This is what I get for giving in to my impulses, she thought as she set the vase back down on the table and knelt to pick up the scattered petals.

The truth was, Prue didn't know why she'd been seized with a sudden desire to foretell the future of her love life by ripping apart innocent members of the flower kingdom. Particularly since she didn't have one. A love life, that is. The three

Halliwell sisters might be very different when it came to goals and temperament, but one thing they all had in common was a bumpy ride when it came to romance. All three girls had had major man trouble at some point in their recent past.

They had a couple of other things in common, too.

They were all dark haired with high cheekbones.

And they were all witches—each with her own special ability. Prue had the power of telekinesis, Piper the ability to freeze time, and Phoebe the ability to see into both the past and the future along with the power of astral projection.

The Halliwells were the Charmed Ones. When they joined their powers, in the Power of Three, they were among the world's most powerful witches. But having powers—and using them for good—also had a downside. It turned them into magnets for warlocks, demons, and every nasty supernatural creature that could find its way to San Francisco.

As far as Prue was concerned, it made the future—and the present—that much more uncertain. No wonder it was hard to find a steady stream of romance.

Piper knelt down beside Prue to help with the mess, heedless of the fact that such an action could cause extreme wrinkles in her new silk dress. Helping others was Piper's standard operating procedure.

"So, you still haven't explained a thing," Piper reminded her. "Spill!"

"There's nothing to spill," Prue said, keeping her voice cool. Cool was her own standard operating mode.

Piper snorted. "Yeah, right. Then how do you explain the flower petals all over Gram's favorite area rug?"

"I was . . . doing some creative problem solving," Prue said.

Piper gave a quick chuckle of appreciation. "Good save," she acknowledged. "You get full points for that."

Prue tossed the petals she'd just gathered at her sister.

"Not down the front of my dress!" Piper protested as she batted the white petals away. "I do not want your problems stuck to my silk."

"My humblest apologies," Prue replied.

Piper frowned. "While you were problem solving, I think you left out a step," she said.

Prue smirked. "What step is that?"

"Before you can figure out if *he* loves you or loves you not, don't you sort of have to have a he?" Piper asked.

Bingo, Prue thought. She was definitely he-less at the moment. That was the problem. "What makes you so smart all of a sudden?" she asked.

"Born that way," Piper said simply. "Can't help myself."

Prue dumped her handful of petals onto the

coffee table, then sat down on the floor and leaned her back against the couch.

"Piper," she said, her tone contemplative. "Do you ever think about what life would be like if we *hadn't* become the Charmed Ones?"

Piper was silent for a moment. She added the petals she'd collected to Prue's and joined her on the floor. "Sometimes," she admitted. "There doesn't seem to be much point, though. There's no going back." She paused. "Besides, we always were the Charmed Ones, Prue. We just didn't always know it." Piper cast a sidelong glance at Prue. "Is that what all this is about?" she asked, gesturing toward the pile of petals.

"Maybe," Prue acknowledged.

It had been Phoebe, the youngest Halliwell, who'd been the first to discover the sisters' secret, Prue recalled. Not long after the threesome had moved back into Halliwell Manor, the big San Francisco Victorian where they'd grown up.

Sometimes, Prue still found it all hard to believe. She kept thinking she'd wake up one morning to find everything the way it used to be—back to what she used to consider normal.

It hadn't happened yet. And if Prue wanted proof it never would, all she had to do was go upstairs to the attic and look at *The Book of Shadows.* It was Phoebe's discovery of this ancient book of spells and her reciting one of its incantations that had awakened the Halliwells' dormant powers.

Time, though, had proved that *The Book of*

Shadows was more than a collection of spells and incantations. It was a direct link with the Halliwells' witch ancestors. It contained all their knowledge about the evil the sisters would be called upon to fight.

Each of them understood that their power was to be used for exactly that purpose: to fight evil and protect the innocent.

Which didn't make getting a date any easier.

"I guess I'm just tired of everything feeling like a battle," Prue tried to explain. "Even stuff that used to seem so simple."

"When was dealing with guys ever simple?" Piper asked.

Prue smiled. "You know what I mean. Sometimes I feel I can't even so much as look at a guy without feeling guilty for keeping back the truth about what I am. But mentioning I'm a witch is not exactly something I'm comfortable doing on a first date."

Piper's expression grew impish. "Along with certain other things."

Prue grinned and bopped her with one of the throw pillows on the couch. Piper retaliated with a few of the daisy petals, then held up her hands. "Truce!" she called out.

The sisters turned toward a familiar sound—the slamming of the front door.

"I'm home," Phoebe's voice called out. She bounded into the living room, bringing a blast of chilly October air with her. Her cheeks were glowing, and her dark brown eyes were sparkling.

"You guys, wait till I tell you my news!" she said.

Prue glanced at her watch. Phoebe was at least twenty minutes late, late enough to put them in danger of losing their dinner reservation. Still, Prue decided, it was hard to feel annoyed with Phoebe when she looked so excited. "What's the news?" she asked.

Phoebe shrugged out of her coat, tossed it onto the couch, and dropped down next to Piper.

"This!" she said. She flourished a piece of paper in the air, then dropped it in Prue's lap.

Prue picked it up. " 'Is Russian Hill Cursed? by Phoebe Halliwell,' " she read aloud. She glanced at her sister. "What is this, Phoebs?"

"You left out the important part," Phoebe said, pointing to the handwritten, bright red A at the top of the paper. " 'A, an excellent treatment of the legend,' " she read proudly.

"Is this like, a school paper?" Piper asked.

Phoebe rolled her eyes. "That's exactly what it is. I've been taking a continuing-ed class at the community college. It's called Legends and Folklore: Uncovering Supernatural San Francisco."

"You?" Prue couldn't help asking. Of all the things Phoebe could get excited about, a college class would never have been Prue's guess.

"Is that so weird?" Phoebe asked more than a bit defensively.

"Well, actually—" Piper started to say.

"Okay, okay, I've never been Miss Academic Achievement," Phoebe admitted. "But the minute I saw this class in the catalog, I just knew I had to take it. It's all about uncovering the roots of local myths and legends about witchcraft and the supernatural in San Francisco."

"You can get credit for stuff like that?" Piper asked.

"That's the best part," Phoebe said. "I figured that for once I could take a class I might actually be good at, *and* it counts toward my degree!"

"That's great," Prue said. "But why the big secret? Why didn't you tell us you were taking a class?"

Phoebe winced. "Part of me was afraid I wouldn't be able to cut it. So I decided to see how I did on my first paper before making any big announcements."

"Looks like you did just fine," Piper said.

Phoebe grinned. "Yeah, I'm a natural." She sat back against the couch with a sigh of satisfaction. All of a sudden, a strange expression flitted across her face. "Um, you guys. Can I ask you a question?"

"Of course," Prue answered.

"How come we're sitting on the floor?"

Surprised, Prue laughed. She cast a quick glance at Piper. Piper gave a tiny nod.

"Because it was there," the two elder Halliwells answered in unison.

Phoebe gave a groan and buried her head in her hands.

"Low blood sugar," she pronounced. "I recognize the symptoms." She scrambled to her feet and held a hand out to Prue. "Come on," she said. "I know this great new sushi place. If we hurry we can just beat the rush."

"You told us about it last week," Prue said as she let Phoebe pull her to her feet. "That's why we made reservations for six-thirty."

"We did?" Phoebe said as she pulled Piper up next. "Excellent. But it's after six-fifteen. We really ought to go. We don't want to lose our reservations."

Prue and Piper rolled their eyes at each other.

"Go ahead and back the car out," Prue told Piper. "I'll be there in a minute."

While her sisters went out to the car, Prue carried the petals and ruined bouquet of daisies into the kitchen and disposed of them in the trash.

She hadn't seen into the future of her love life, but the prospect no longer bothered her as much as it had earlier. Somehow, it would all work out, even if at this moment Prue couldn't see how. Somewhere out there was the right guy for her. She just wished he'd hurry up and show himself!

In the meantime, there was the evening with her sisters to look forward to, she realized as she hurried through the living room and grabbed her coat. Her sisters, the one constant in her totally unpredictable life.

* * *

"Going once. Going twice. Sold to Mr. Dylan Thomas!" the morning auctioneer at Buckland's shouted.

At her post near the front of the crowded auction room, Prue waited while the buyer made his way toward her. She couldn't help feeling a bit of envy. He'd just bought a chair that she coveted. Still, Prue gave him her brightest smile.

"You purchased the William Morris chair," she said as he handed her the number that identified him. "Congratulations, Mister—"

As she found his name on her list, Prue frowned. The guy's named was Dylan Thomas. Why did that sound familiar?

"I'm afraid that actually is my name," he said.

Prue blinked. Had she spoken her thought aloud?

"Beg your pardon?" she said.

The guy in front of her gave her an engaging smile. Prue blinked again, but this time it wasn't because she was confused. It was because Dylan Thomas was gorgeous. Dark hair swept back from a high forehead, then tumbled down just far enough to flirt with his shirt collar. His mouth was a study in contrasts, somehow managing to be thin and sensuous all at the same time.

His clothes kept the contrast going: a sleek black jacket topped a pair of dark jeans and a white linen shirt. The whole effect reminded Prue of a romantic poet.

But it was his eyes that really had Prue's pulse

hopping up and down like a kindergartner on Christmas morning. They were a deep mesmerizing blue, like the waters of Lake Tahoe.

"My name," he explained. "I'm afraid it really is Dylan Thomas."

Prue could feel her face start to color. She hadn't meant to be so obvious. What was wrong with her? "I was just wondering why it sounded so familiar," she admitted.

"I get that reaction all the time," Dylan Thomas said with an easy smile. "It's all my mother's fault. She was an English major who spent her honeymoon in Wales in the famous poet Dylan Thomas's hometown. When I arrived exactly nine months later—"

"She didn't have a choice," Prue put in. "She had to name you for Wales's most celebrated poet!" She smiled. She decided that she liked the name. It was romantic and sophisticated all at the same time.

Dylan Thomas's eyes sparkled, sending her pulse racing. He leaned over the podium, pointing at Prue's list. "Now, about my antique chair, Miss—Mrs.—Ms.—"

Smooth, Prue thought. A very smooth way of finding out whether or not she was single. She made a split-second decision.

"Miss," she said. "Halliwell. Prue Halliwell."

Dylan's eyes suddenly shone a little more blue, something Prue would have sworn was absolutely impossible.

"About my chair, *Miss* Prue Halliwell," he said. "I saw the way you looked at it. Sorry, but it won't do you a bit of good. I bought it and it's mine now."

Prue felt her color rise once more. He was right about how she felt about the chair, she realized. Her job at Buckland's brought her into daily contact with countless beautiful and unusual objects. Few, however, spoke to her the way this chair had, with its graceful, simple lines, rich wood frame, and gorgeous woven upholstery. She almost felt as if it had been designed just for her.

"You're right. I have been admiring it," she admitted.

"Well, don't think of it as gone," Dylan said. He leaned a little closer, his vivid eyes glowing. "You can always visit it, you know."

Prue laughed. This guy was totally amazing. She felt as if he had just read her mind. Or maybe he was just specially tuned in to her.

Either way, he was definitely exciting.

"Ahem."

Prue jumped, startled, and was amazed to see three people had formed a line to one side of her podium. While she and Dylan had been talking, the auction had continued and now there were clients waiting to have their purchases verified. Prue hadn't even noticed them.

What on earth is the matter with me? she wondered again. She always stayed on top of things. Always.

Instantly, Dylan switched gears, as if he realized his behavior could get Prue into trouble.

"I apologize if I kept you waiting," he said to the older man standing behind him. "I'm afraid I found Miss Halliwell so interesting, I took up more than my fair share of her time."

"Can't say as I blame you," the man replied with a wink.

Prue felt herself blushing like crazy. Dylan Thomas was not what she needed to focus on right now, but she couldn't help herself. As she started to help the next customer her eyes darted toward him.

She watched as he stepped back, then took a small pad from his inside jacket pocket and began to write on it.

A few minutes later as she signed another customer's verification form, Dylan slipped a note in front of her.

Prue—

I can see I'd better go. If I stay, I'll want to distract you. But I've got to see you again. How about this weekend? Please say yes.

Dylan

Prue forgot all about the customer standing in front of her. She gazed up into Dylan's dark blue eyes. "Yes," she said.

Dylan flashed his thousand-watt smile at her. "A Morris chair and a date with the most beautiful woman in San Francisco," he said softly. "Sometimes I can't believe my luck."

Prue felt herself blushing. She was seriously beginning to feel as if she was being swept off her feet, and the truth was, she liked it.

"Listen," Dylan went on, sounding a bit hesitant. "About this weekend. On Saturday night my band is playing at this great new club. I'd really love it if you were there. So how would you feel about coming to the gig?"

"That'd be great," Prue said. "Where are you playing?"

"I'll call and leave the address on your voice mail," Dylan told her. He backed away, his eyes full of promise. "Until this weekend."

The customer standing in front of Prue cleared his throat impatiently. "Excuse me," he said, "but when will I be able to pick up my painting?"

"You can take this receipt to the second floor and—" Prue began to explain, but her mind was on Dylan Thomas and the miraculous fact that she had just said yes to a date.

For once she hadn't worried or tried to plan for the future. She'd stayed in the moment. Of course, the fact that the moment had included Dylan made it pretty easy, but still. It was a change, and Prue figured every little bit counted. Wait until she told Piper!

Was this what it felt like to finally meet her own special someone?

* * *

Later that afternoon Piper stood on the empty stage of her club, P3, attempting to glare at the young man who'd just walked in. She put her hands on her hips and tried to make herself look stern. "You're late," she said in the most severe tone she could manage. Once again, she realized, she was doing a pretty poor job.

But then, it was hard to sound tough, she thought, when you were talking to an absolute Adonis.

The guy standing in front of her, holding a guitar case and gazing up at her with a look that managed to be both apologetic and completely confident, was one of the most amazingly gorgeous guys she'd ever seen. Though looks alone didn't account for his incredible appeal. Something about him just seemed to draw her in. He had the perfect combination of man-about-town sophistication and little-boy charm.

She'd noticed it first over the phone when he'd called to see if he could book his band into her nightclub. Piper had been impressed that he'd called himself. Most bands had their managers make the arrangements. But the founder and lead singer of Dylan and the Good Nights said he preferred to handle bookings himself. It gave him a chance to get to know the club owners.

Piper certainly wouldn't mind getting to know Dylan better.

The Good Nights were a swing band, perfect for the current craze for swing dancing, and they didn't do just instrumentals—they did vocals, too. Dylan was their lead singer. Piper had thought he'd sounded great on the demo tape he'd sent. Plus she'd loved the name of the band, the perfect in-joke on the lead singer's name, which just happened to be Dylan Thomas, like the poet who'd written, "Do not go gentle into that good night."

"You're right," Dylan said now. "I'm late and there's no excuse. I'm really sorry, Piper. I can call you Piper, can't I? I mean—you are Piper Halliwell, aren't you? This is your club, isn't it?"

A self-deprecating smile crossed his face. "Oh, I'm making a terrible mess of this, aren't I?"

Actually, Piper thought, he was being pretty adorable.

"You haven't made a mess yet," she said, relenting just a little. "But we run on a pretty tight schedule around here. I need you to finish your sound check before I let my after-work crowd in, Mr. Thomas."

"Please," he murmured, "I wish you'd call me Dylan."

"All right," Piper answered. "As I said over the phone—Dylan—P3 usually does live music only on the weekends. My weekday regulars are used to being able to come right on in. I'm happy to give you a couple of extra nights to check out the space and do some practice sets, but not if you disrupt my business."

"Right." Dylan nodded, his expression serious. "I completely understand. I'll get right on the sound check. Won't be more than a couple more minutes." He took a few steps toward the stage, then turned back. "Um—Piper?"

Piper turned and saw a shy, hopeful look in his eyes. Really, this guy was just too adorable!

"You'll be around later, right? Maybe I can buy you a drink or something between sets? You know, to apologize. I'd really like that."

"I'd like that, too," she told him.

He gave her a smile so dazzling Piper was afraid the glare would give her permanent eye damage. Then he turned and hurried to the band platform.

This guy could definitely spell trouble, Piper thought. In an entirely good way, of course. She could hardly wait to get home to tell her sisters all about him!

CHAPTER 2

"Is anybody sitting here?" a voice beside Phoebe asked.

Phoebe was early for her Tuesday evening class, her notebook already open on her desk. Only one other student, an older woman named Marjorie Yarnell, had gotten there earlier.

Marjorie, who sat in the seat next to her, was always the first one in class. And as always, she looked impeccable: perfectly frosted blond hair, elegant clothing, expensive jewelry. Phoebe had been curious about Marjorie since the first day of class. She was so not your typical community college student. But then, an interest in the supernatural definitely crossed age and economic barriers.

"Didn't you hear me? I asked if anyone was sitting here?"

Phoebe started and glanced up at a skinny guy whose name she could never remember. He was more typical of the class: young, probably right out of high school, if the slight case of acne decorating his forehead was any indication.

Phoebe opened her mouth to say the seat was open, when another voice interrupted her, saying, "Sorry, it's saved."

The young guy flushed scarlet, then scurried away as another classmate, Brett Weir, slid into the seat on the other side of her. Brett seemed closer to Phoebe's age, maybe a couple of years older. He gave her what he obviously hoped was a winning smile.

"Phoebe, right?" he said. "I'm Brett." He held out his hand.

Wonder what his ultimate career goal is? Phoebe thought. Her insta-guess would have to be something along the lines of used-car salesman.

She shook his hand briefly. She didn't want to be rude, but she didn't want to encourage him, either. She was in this class to study, not to flirt. This was the launch of her new college career, and getting a good grade was what mattered.

As Phoebe released Brett Weir's hand, a girl slid into the seat behind him. Phoebe recognized her as Wendy Chang. Weren't Brett and Wendy going out? Phoebe remembered Wendy clinging to Brett's arm just the week before. Now Wendy glared at Phoebe, then she quickly turned her attention to Brett.

"Hi, Brett," she said as other students filtered in.

Brett mumbled something Phoebe couldn't quite catch, then turned his back.

Uh-oh, she thought. What happened there? It looked like major relationship trouble, which Phoebe didn't need to know any more about, thank you very much. Not only was she not in the class to flirt, she definitely wasn't in it to get involved in other people's problems. This class was business only.

Professor Hagin, a man with a deep dramatic voice, strode to the front of the room. "All right, class," he said. "If everyone is settled, let's get started." He paused for a moment, fumbling in the chalk tray.

Professor Hagin was tall with a shock of wild gray hair. After managing to fill the air with an astonishing amount of chalk dust, he finally found an actual piece and began writing on the board behind him. He was definitely chalk-challenged, Phoebe thought, but he was also the best teacher she'd ever had.

"Now," Professor Hagin said, rubbing his hands together, and revealing what he'd written: "The Legend of the Halloween Murders."

"Since Halloween is coming up this Sunday, I thought it would be appropriate to discuss one of San Francisco's many unsolved mysteries, one that happened right here, on this very campus. Is anyone familiar with the legend of the Halloween Murders?"

No one answered, though Phoebe swore she could feel the room hum with anticipation. She uncapped her pen and got set to take notes.

"Then let me tell you about them," Professor Hagin said. He sat down on the edge of his desk, swinging one leg back and forth.

"The Halloween Murders occurred more than forty years ago, in 1958. At that time this school wasn't a community college, as it is now. It was a private university, catering to the wealthy young people of Northern California.

"One of the school's most popular girls was Betty Warren. The legend likes to make much of the fact that Betty could have had any guy she wanted. But she didn't choose a guy from her own social background. Instead, she fell in love with a scholarship student named Ronald Galvez.

"Betty's family and most of her friends disapproved, including Betty's best friend, Charlotte Logan. But she refused to let that stop her. Betty Warren loved Ronald Galvez."

I think I like Betty, Phoebe thought as she jotted down the names of the key participants in the story. It took courage to stand up for what you wanted. What would it feel like to have to defend your love against your friends and family?

"There are those who insist that Betty and Ronald's relationship would have ended sooner or later," Professor Hagin went on. "But even they couldn't have predicted that it would end in tragedy. On Halloween night in 1958, Betty and Ronald both died under circumstances which were horrifying and are still shrouded in mystery."

Look out, here it comes, Phoebe thought. She found herself leaning forward, literally on the edge of her seat.

"There was a party that night—a costume party, naturally. It was held in Thayer Hall, now the Student Union. Back then it was a dormitory. Betty and Ronald showed up at the party, danced together, and then went into a back room—I probably don't have to tell you what for—"

A titter of laughter swept the classroom.

"Moments later screams interrupted the party. Betty staggered out from the back room where she'd gone with Ronald, covered in blood. She collapsed upon the floor, multiple stab wounds covering her body.

"When the partygoers rushed to the back room, they found Ronald, with blood on his clothing. At his feet, Betty's best friend, Charlotte, lay sprawled. She was dead of a stab wound to the stomach. Ronald hysterically insisted he wasn't responsible for what had happened, but no one believed him—because in his hands he was clutching a bloody butcher's knife."

Professor Hagin certainly did know how to tell a story, Phoebe thought as she struggled against the shiver that wanted to work its way down her spine.

"Some of the students at the party tried to grab

hold of Ronald," the professor continued, "but he held them off with the knife and escaped out a window. Eventually, he was hunted down and cornered by the police. When he tried to flee again, he was gunned down. Betty's uncle was the chief of police. He'd given his officers instructions to shoot to kill.

"The legend says that, with his dying words, Ronald called out for Betty and continued to profess his innocence. The legend also says that the spirits of all three young people who died that night—Betty, Ronald, and Charlotte—continue to haunt this campus, restless because of their horrific and untimely ends. Although the case was closed and Ronald Galvez officially held responsible for the deaths, no one has ever investigated his dying claim of innocence."

The story really is a tragedy, Phoebe thought. Not only did three young people lose their lives, but Betty's powerful family made sure that Ronald took the blame.

But what if he hadn't been responsible? Phoebe wondered. What if something else had happened that night? Something hidden for all these years, unexplained—unaccounted for?

Phoebe's attention snapped back to the present as she noticed that Marjorie Yarnell had gone pale, and the hand that held her pen was shaking badly.

"Are you all right?" Phoebe whispered. Instinctively, she reached out and touched the older woman's shoulder.

"I'm fine!" Marjorie said, sounding startled.

But Phoebe wasn't fine. No sooner had she touched Marjorie, than she'd felt the jolt that always meant a vision was coming on. Seconds later the edges of her vision went fuzzy. Images danced before her eyes, then focused abruptly, as if she were looking into a telescope.

She could see a large room decorated with black crepe paper and jack-o'-lanterns. It was crowded, filled with young people in Halloween costumes. They were laughing, dancing together to an old fifties' song, until an unearthly scream cut across the sound of the music. The scream was so horrifying, it was all Phoebe could do not to clap her hands over her ears.

The sound of the scream jerked her back to the present. Once more she was sitting in the classroom, staring at Professor Hagin.

Shakily, Phoebe looked around. As usual, her vision had lasted no more than a few seconds. Also as usual, those few seconds had been totally unsettling. Phoebe didn't think any of the other students had noticed her strange trip back to the scene of the murders. They all looked intrigued and excited, except for Marjorie Yarnell. She looked as if she was about to faint.

Why did touching Marjorie set off the vision? Phoebe asked herself. Was it simply because Marjorie had been alive at the time of the murders? Or was it something more than that?

As Professor Hagin turned to write something

else on the chalkboard, Phoebe leaned over to Marjorie. "Are you sure you're okay?" she murmured.

Marjorie nodded, but Phoebe noticed her bottom lip trembling.

"It's just that it's such a gruesome story," Marjorie said in a low voice. "Somehow, I hadn't expected the legends we studied would be quite so . . . graphic."

"It *was* pretty intense," Phoebe agreed.

Professor Hagin continued the lecture, which included a list of the best times and places to get a view of the ghosts of Betty, Ronald, and Charlotte.

"Now that I've stirred your interest with the legend," Professor Hagin said at the end of the class period, "let me tell you that the Halloween Murders present you with your first opportunity for extra credit. Anyone volunteering to do a special project on the hauntings will receive extra points, which will count toward your final grade. Do I have any volunteers?"

Phoebe's hand shot skyward.

The story was absolutely perfect for her, she thought. She'd already had a vision about it. Who had a better chance of unraveling the secrets of the past? Besides, she thought, surely the best way to prove her seriousness about doing well in the course was to sign up for extra credit.

Maybe her powers would help her do something really special, like finally prove or disprove

Ronald Galvez's claim of innocence. That ought to guarantee her a good grade.

Phoebe fluttered her fingers eagerly.

"Very well, Ms. Halliwell," Professor Hagin said, nodding. "You may take this assignment for extra credit."

Beside Phoebe, Brett Weir suddenly waved his hand. "I'd like to work on it, too, Professor Hagin," he called out.

"Such enthusiasm," Professor Hagin murmured, but he smiled and said, "Perhaps you and Ms. Halliwell would care to work together, Mr. Weir? You could pool your resources."

"That's fine by me," Brett said, his expression brightening.

"Ms. Halliwell?" Professor Hagin queried.

Phoebe nodded. "Okay."

Having Brett for a partner wasn't necessarily her first choice. Phoebe had a feeling he was going to prove more interested in getting to know her than in solving the mystery, but she was sure that she could handle him.

Besides, two heads *were* better than one, and it would be great to have someone else to help with the general research.

Phoebe saw Wendy Chang scowl at her. "I want to work on it, too," Wendy spoke up.

Professor Hagin held up his hands, as if to ward off the sudden flow of student interest.

"I think two students on this project is enough," he said. "There will be plenty of other opportunities for extra credit this semester. If you—"

But whatever the professor was about to say was cut off as the bell rang.

Wow! Phoebe thought. Professor Hagin's retelling of the events of 1958 had been so compelling, she'd hardly noticed how fast the class period had gone by.

Quickly, she recapped her pen, swept it and her notebook into her shoulder bag, and got to her feet. She could hardly wait to formulate her plan of attack. Maybe she'd head to the Student Union, grab a quick cup of coffee, and make a list of possible avenues to investigate before she went home.

She turned, heading for the door, when a hand on her arm brought her to a halt. She was surprised to see Marjorie Yarnell looking even more upset than she'd been in class.

"Phoebe," Marjorie began. "You probably think I'm just a silly old woman—"

"I don't," Phoebe protested. "Not at all." But I do wonder what's going on with you, she added silently. What got you in such a state?

"It's just . . ." Marjorie hesitated. "Be careful when you investigate those murders, will you?"

"Of course I will," Phoebe answered, this time totally mystified by Marjorie's request. The murders had happened over forty years ago. Phoebe couldn't see how researching them now would endanger anyone.

"Well," Marjorie said a little awkwardly. She took her hand from Phoebe's arm and picked up her elegant leather book satchel. "I guess that's all right, then."

Then she strode briskly from the classroom, leaving a puzzled Phoebe staring after her.

Maybe she's just freaked out by the whole ghost thing, Phoebe thought. As in, the possibility of being on the same campus with them. Maybe that's why she set off my vision.

As she made her way out of the classroom and into the hallway, Phoebe wondered if it was possible that anyone had actually seen the ghosts. Was anything ever reported about them in the campus newspaper? That was one area she'd want to investigate. After all, there might not even be any specters.

"Phoebe!" a voice behind her said. Now what? Phoebe thought. She turned and saw Wendy Chang was standing just behind her. She did not look like a happy camper.

Wendy's eyes were hot and angry. Her mouth was tight and pinched. "Brett's not the nice guy you think he is," she said abruptly. "If you know what's good for you, you'll watch your step with him."

"Singing my praises again, Wendy?" Brett's sarcastic voice asked.

What am I? A weird-behavior magnet? Phoebe wondered. She totally did not need this.

Wendy flushed scarlet. She clutched her book

bag to her chest. "Just remember what I said," she told Phoebe. Then she hurried off down the hallway and disappeared into a crowd of students.

"I'm really sorry about that, Phoebe," Brett Weir said. He fell into step beside her as Phoebe let the crush of students move her down the corridor. "Wendy and I used to go out."

"Don't tell me. But you just recently broke up," Phoebe said.

Brett gave her a somewhat sheepish grin. "Got it in one," he said. "The truth is, Wendy was a little"—he paused as if searching for just the right word—"*intense* for my taste," he finally said.

"Actually," he went on, "I think her behavior was pretty obsessive. If I even said 'excuse me' to another girl Wendy would totally freak. I just couldn't deal with that."

Great, Phoebe thought. Marvelous. Peachy. First she was warned off her extra-credit assignment, and now she was dealing with the jealous ex of a guy she wasn't even interested in. Some girls just had all the luck.

"Thanks for letting me know. I'll try to steer clear," she told Brett.

"Well, that'll be tough," he said. "I mean, we are going to be working together. And Wendy won't like that. Hey, do you think we should exchange phone numbers or something? So we can get in touch if anything really important comes up?"

Nice try, Phoebe thought, even if it wasn't very

subtle. Actually, under other circumstances, she might have allowed herself to get interested in Brett. He was kind of cute, with big brown eyes and hair that flopped across his forehead. He sort of reminded Phoebe of a friendly puppy.

Now, though, she couldn't let anything distract her from her goal of a good grade. This class was the kick-off of her new college career, and she wasn't about to let anything spoil it, not even cute, friendly Brett Weir.

"You know, Brett," she said. "I don't think so. My sisters and I try to keep the home line free for family stuff."

He looked so crestfallen, that Phoebe relented, just a little. "I'll meet with you tomorrow, though," she said. "Let's each come up with a list of things about the legend to investigate, then meet for coffee to compare them and divide them up."

"Great idea," Brett said. "I knew we'd make a good team." He reached out to put an arm around her shoulders.

"See you tomorrow, then," Phoebe said as she slid out of range. Without looking back, she hurried off down the corridor.

Brother! She'd figured going back to school would be a challenge, but she thought it would be because of the academic challenge, not the behavior of her fellow students.

Phoebe checked her watch. All that after-class conversation had taken longer than she'd planned. Instead of heading to the Student Union, she'd just head for home. She did her best thinking there anyway. Maybe she'd light an inspiration aromatherapy candle while she formulated her plan of attack. She could even get some input from Prue and Piper.

Though, really, Phoebe thought as she headed for her car, she wanted to handle solving the mystery of the Halloween Murders on her own. It would be a great way to prove to herself *and* to her sisters that she was more than just "the flaky Halliwell."

She reached her car, unlocked it, tossed her books onto the passenger side, and slid behind the wheel. It wasn't until she actually had the key in the ignition that Phoebe noticed the white piece of paper, fluttering against her windshield.

Is somebody trying to sell me something? she wondered. She was reaching for the wiper switch to whoosh it away when a gust of wind blew the paper flat against the windshield. Phoebe's hand froze in midair. Now the message on the paper was clear.

"Watch your step," it said, in bold, black letters.

Phoebe yanked her keys from the ignition, got out, and snatched the piece of paper. Then she slammed the door behind her, crumpled the piece of paper into a ball in one tight fist, and strode to the edge of the parking lot where she dumped it in a trash can.

If Wendy Chang thinks she can get me with cheap scare tactics, she's got another think coming, Phoebe thought as she stomped back to the car. She thrust her key into the lock, turned it, then gave the door a swift tug.

It wouldn't open.

Phoebe pulled again. The door stayed closed. She could feel panic rising like bile in the back of her throat.

This is ridiculous, she thought. I've just got to calm down. She took two deep breaths and realized what the problem was. The car door had locked.

She put the key into the lock, turned it in the other direction, and opened the door without a problem. She slid behind the wheel, took a third breath, then put the key in the ignition and started the engine. Her hands trembled ever so slightly as she put the car in gear. Phoebe ignored them.

Why worry about ghosts? she thought as she eased from her parking spot. I've got a real-live drama going on right here in this time zone—complete with an unpredictable villain in the form of the scorned and desperate Wendy Chang.

CHAPTER 3

"Have you seen this?" Phoebe asked, holding out an orange flyer that announced the first campus Halloween Party in over forty years.

It was Wednesday afternoon, and she and Brett were having coffee in the Student Union, which had once been Thayer Hall, the scene of the Halloween murders. When the campus had been changed from a private university to a community college, the dorms had been remodeled and converted to other functions. Some administrator had decided to make Thayer as public a place as possible.

Phoebe was torn between thinking this was kind of creepy and thinking it was brilliant.

Turning Thayer into a place where all sorts of students with all sorts of different kinds of energy gathered was certainly one way of attempting to blow away the psychic cobwebs of the past.

Brett glanced at the flyer and nodded. "Yeah, I saw it," he said. "I hear they're still looking for people to help with the decorations, the night before the party. They're going to do a fifties theme. Great idea, huh?"

What are you, nuts? Phoebe almost said. Instead, she settled for, "Well, I don't know if I'd go that far."

Hosting a Halloween costume party in the same building where the murders had taken place didn't sound like a great idea. At the worst, it sounded potentially dangerous. At best it sounded . . . just plain tacky.

Phoebe folded the flyer and tucked it into her book bag. She took a sip of latte and said, "I've been thinking about possible areas for us to research. We should find out if there have ever been any reports of strange incidents in or around Thayer. Other than the murders themselves, I mean."

Brett's brow wrinkled. "What are you driving at?"

"I was just thinking we could use the ghost angle as a way to approach the mystery," Phoebe explained. "After all, the extra credit is supposed to be about the hauntings. We could check old school newspapers for unexplained occurrences around the scene of the crime in the years since the murders, that sort of thing."

"Wow!" Brett said, his puppy dog eyes growing enormous. "That's a great idea! I never even thought of that. I was thinking more along the lines of trying to figure out what really happened, you know, stuff like that."

That was a good idea, too, Phoebe had to admit. In fact, she'd already thought of it.

"I think we should explore both options, don't you?" she asked.

Brett nodded vigorously. "Definitely," he said. "Want me to handle the ghost thing?"

"That'd be totally great, Brett," Phoebe said.

Things were working out just the way she'd hoped they would. While Brett spent time in the library with the microfiche, she'd tackle the first item on the to-do list she'd made. It was an item Phoebe definitely wanted to handle herself.

"What are you going to do?" Brett asked.

In answer, Phoebe pulled a thick book out of her book bag. It was a college yearbook from 1959. "I couldn't find the 1958 yearbook," she said, "but I found the one from the year after. And inside I discovered this." She flipped the yearbook open and pointed to a picture.

"Wow!" Brett said. "Is that wild or what?" He read the caption aloud, " 'John Williams, Valedictorian of the Class of 1959; Varsity Football, linebacker.' "

Brett grinned and added, "And currently, Professor Williams, Dean of Student Affairs. I'm going to interview the current college staff members who were also students here at the time of the murders. Starting at the top."

"What can I do for you, Ms. Halliwell?" Dean Williams asked later that afternoon.

Phoebe sat up straighter in the hard-backed chair in his office. Something about the dean of Student Affairs was intimidating. Even if she hadn't already read it in the yearbook, Phoebe would have guessed that he had been a football player. He was built big and square, sort of like a walking refrigerator, she thought. His manner was straightforward and gruff.

"I'm writing a paper for Professor Hagin's class," she began. "On the Halloween Murders. Since you were here then, I thought you might know what actually happened."

A dark expression crossed the dean's face, and Phoebe wondered if she'd asked the wrong question.

"Or maybe you knew Ronald Galvez or Betty Warren?" she tried.

Dean Williams leaned forward, resting his elbows on his large oak desk. "Betty Warren was a friend of mine. One of the nicest girls you could ever meet. There's no doubt in my mind that Ronald Galvez killed her and Charlotte," he added in a tone that defied anyone to argue with him. "That boy always was trouble, right from the get-go."

Phoebe made a record of Dean Williams's comments in her notebook. His opinion really came as no surprise. He'd already admitted he was one of Betty's friends—one who disapproved of her relationship with Ronald.

"How was Ronald trouble?" Phoebe asked, curious.

"Galvez was your classic bad boy. He was smart enough—that's how he got the scholarship—but he had a real chip on his shoulder. He was always taking dares, getting into fights. He was nothing like Betty's other friends."

"Wasn't there anybody who supported Ron and Betty's relationship?" Phoebe asked.

"Absolutely not," Dean Williams told her. "Of course, the person most upset about it was Betty's best friend, Charlotte Logan. She couldn't bear to see Betty throwing herself away on a guy like Ron Galvez. She knew they were headed for trouble, but nothing Charlotte said could change Betty's mind."

An expression Phoebe couldn't quite read flickered across the dean's features. "The truth is," he went on, almost to himself, "Betty could be kind of stubborn."

Instantly, Phoebe felt her senses start to prickle. There was something about the look on Dean Williams's face when he spoke about Betty. He was a year younger than she was, it was true, but was it possible that he once had a crush on her?

"My theory has always been that something Charlotte was saying finally got through to Betty the night of the party," he explained. "I think that Betty went into that room with Ronald to break up with him.

"I've never agreed with the theory that Betty went into that room with Ronald to 'fool around,' " Dean Williams went on, his face coloring ever so slightly. "She just wasn't that kind of girl."

Gotcha! Phoebe thought. Suddenly she had a pretty good idea of why John Williams was acting so strangely about this case. He did have a crush on Betty Warren all those years ago. He displayed the most classic symptom of all: denial about her and any other guy.

"So you think that when Betty told Ronald they were through, he killed her?" Phoebe asked.

"I'm sure of it," Dean Williams said. "Betty told him she wanted out, and he went insane and murdered her. And I think Charlotte tried to stop him, so he turned on her as well. He probably believed she was responsible for the breakup."

"That's very interesting," Phoebe said as she finished adding the dean's theory to her notebook. Then she glanced up. Dean Williams was looking perfectly at ease behind his big oak desk. Maybe even a little smug, Phoebe thought.

She figured it was time to do the other thing she'd come here for: stir the pot. Bring up her alternative version of what might have happened and see what kind of reaction she got.

"You don't think somebody else could have been involved, do you?" she asked Dean Williams, watching him closely. "Someone who got out of the room before the others arrived? A person whose identity has never been discovered?"

At Phoebe's words, Dean Williams's face turned beet red. He shot up from his desk chair as if fired from a canon.

"That's nothing but ridiculous speculation," he all but shouted. "Ronald Galvez's family tried to suggest some such nonsense at the time, but no one believed them. You've no business bringing such an idea back up now. It's far too late."

He came around the side of the desk, and Phoebe got nervously to her feet, fumbling with her pen and notebook. "I'm afraid that's all the time I can give you, Ms. Halliwell," the dean said. He gestured at the door and Phoebe scurried toward it. She had her hand on the knob when Dean Williams spoke once again.

"Take my advice, Ms. Halliwell," he said in a quiet voice that had the hairs on the back of Phoebe's neck standing on end. "Don't stir up trouble looking for mysteries where none exist. This case was solved over forty years ago. Ronald Galvez killed those two girls."

"Thanks for your time, Dean Williams," Phoebe managed to get out. Then she pulled open the door and scooted through it, her thoughts whirling.

What had really just happened in there? Phoebe

closed the door behind her, then stopped short. Marjorie Yarnell was standing right in front of her.

"Oh, Phoebe. I—I didn't see you there—" Marjorie said.

Well, of course you didn't see me, Phoebe thought. I've just come out of the dean's office.

Marjorie was standing close enough to the door that it was a miracle Phoebe hadn't run her over on her way out.

Was she close enough to have been eavesdropping? Phoebe wondered suddenly.

"I think the dean is free now, if you have an appointment with him," Phoebe said, glancing at the empty desk of his secretary.

Marjorie's hands plucked nervously at her purse strap. "Oh, no," she protested. "It was nothing like that. I—I don't have an appointment with him. I was just sort of in the neighborhood—you know how it is."

Surely one didn't just find one's self in the neighborhood of the dean's outer office, Phoebe thought.

"I'll see you in class, Phoebe dear," Marjorie went on, plainly making an effort to pull herself together. Then she pushed open the outer office door and walked away, her pumps clicking against the hardwood floor.

Whoa! Phoebe thought. First Dean Williams completely freaks at the suggestion that Ronald Galvez wasn't responsible for the murders. Then Marjorie freaks at the mention of Dean Williams!

There had to be more to the story of Betty and Ronald, Phoebe thought as she hurried from the dean's office. Something that he had said came back to her: "The case was solved over forty years ago." Maybe it was time she checked some police records to see just how thoroughly the case had been investigated, especially after Betty's uncle gave a shoot-to-kill order.

Phoebe was determined to uncover the real story of what happened that night—and guarantee herself a terrific grade in the process!

"I really can't thank you enough, Piper. Giving the band these couple of nights for practice sets has been great. I—"

Across the intimate table at P3, Dylan Thomas paused and waited until Piper lifted her lovely dark eyes to his.

It had been just one day since he'd met Piper, but it was a day Dylan had put to excellent use, if he did say so himself.

He held Piper's eyes another moment, then looked down at the table, as if suddenly flustered.

"What is it, Dylan?" Piper asked. "It's all right. You can tell me."

Soon enough, Dylan thought. Soon enough.

He could almost feel the waves of compassion emanating from her. Feel her fingers itch with the need to reach out to his. Well, he could accommodate that little silent request, he thought. It did happen to fit in perfectly with his plan.

He eased his hand onto the table, pretending to reach for his coffee cup, then leaving his hand at loose ends, palm up, at the very last second.

Piper never even hesitated. She slipped her fingers into his at once, giving them a squeeze of reassurance. Dylan squeezed back. He could feel the way her body hummed at the contact.

That was good. It was very, very good. Because it meant he had Piper Halliwell exactly where he wanted her—right in the palm of his hand.

Now it was time for the next step of his plan.

"It's just been so great to have the time to really get comfortable with the acoustics of the club," Dylan said. "It's important for the kind of music we play, and most club owners don't seem to understand that."

He tightened his fingers just a little and was rewarded by the feel of Piper's pulse jumping. "Of course, I should have known you would."

Piper shrugged, as if to dismiss the notion that what she'd done was unusual, though he noticed the way her cheeks turned pink at the compliment.

"The word of mouth your band is generating has been good for business," she said. "Looks like we'll be sold out for every single one of your shows this weekend."

Dylan's brilliant smile flashed. "Excellent," he said. "I've invited a special guest to come on Saturday night. I hope you don't mind."

"Of course not," Piper said.

"Excuse me, I'm sorry to interrupt you."

Dylan and Piper looked up to find one of P3's wait staff standing by their table.

"What is it, Nicole?" Piper asked.

"There's a phone call for you," the young woman answered.

"Sorry." Piper gave him an apologetic smile. "I'll be right back," she promised.

You certainly will, he thought, making sure he maintained the pressure on her fingers while she eased them from his. Really, this is almost too easy, he thought as he watched her follow Nicole back across the club to the bar. The telephone rested on its polished wood surface.

Somehow, he'd have thought the Charmed Ones were smarter than this. Not that he was complaining, of course.

Dylan waited until Piper put the receiver to her ear and settled onto a barstool with her back to him. Then he reached into the inside pocket of his sleek black jacket and withdrew a small velvet pouch. He loosened the drawstring, reached inside, and took out a pinch of violet powder.

He stretched, as if he'd been sitting in one position just a little too long, and dropped the pinch of violet powder into Piper's coffee.

Anyone watching would have seen the air above the coffee cup sparkle strangely for just a moment, first white, then red, then finally an inky black before subsiding entirely.

But no one was watching, of course. Dylan had made sure of that, just as he'd made sure that Piper would be called away from their table when he needed her to be.

"Nothing bad, I hope," he said after she put down the receiver and walked back toward him.

"Nothing at all, actually," Piper said as she sat down again. "By the time I got there, whoever it was had hung up."

"Hmm," Dylan said, raising his coffee cup and taking a sip. "I bet a club gets a lot of crank calls like that."

"Some," Piper agreed, lifting her own cup. She took a sip, then made a face. "I'm going to have to talk to the barista," she said. "This coffee is way too strong."

"Really?" Dylan asked, his tone surprised. Carefully, he set his cup back down. Excellent. She'd taken the bait. Literally. Now it was just a matter of time before the powder he'd put into her coffee began to take effect.

"I hadn't noticed. Mine seems just perfect."

"Well, of course it does," Piper answered without hesitation. "It's yours, after all."

Dylan watched in delight as her mouth dropped open in surprise at what she'd said.

Just about right, he thought. Say, thirty seconds.

"I'm so sorry," Piper said. "I don't usually—"

"Surely you don't expect me to accept that apology," Dylan said with a smile.

His delight increased as a now completely

flustered Piper shot to her feet, bumping against the table and knocking over both cups of coffee.

Better and better, Dylan thought as he, too, got to his feet. Not only had Piper drunk his potion, she'd just destroyed the evidence of it.

"I'd better get this cleaned up," Piper said. "I didn't get any on you, did I?"

Dylan opened his jacket, revealing the body-hugging silk shirt he'd put on underneath. He could almost feel Piper's blood pressure sky-rocket.

"I think I'm okay," he said. He took a step closer. "I'll let you handle things here," he said, his tone soft. "But I'll look forward to seeing you tomorrow, Piper."

"Tomorrow. Yeah, okay, fine," Piper said. Then she scurried away in search of a towel. Dylan couldn't help but wonder how long it was going to take her to find one.

He was humming as he walked through the doors of P3. So far, so good, he thought. He paused on the sidewalk and checked his watch. Four forty-five. For nine-to-five businesses, almost closing time.

He was going to have to move fast if he was going to put the next phase of his plan into action: getting to Prue before she left her office. He'd never make it if he had to battle the rush-hour traffic.

Dylan Thomas closed both eyes in a concen-trated, deliberate blink. He opened his eyes to find himself standing outside the front entrance of Buckland's.

Fortunately, as a warlock, he had other means of transportation at his disposal.

"Come on, Prue," he coaxed five minutes later. "You can't make me believe you don't have time for one measly cup of coffee." He leaned across her desk. "I'll tell you where I put the chair," he teased.

One side of Prue's mouth quirked up. "Something tells me it's in your apartment."

"Hotel suite," he corrected her.

"Hotel suite," she repeated.

"Who told you?" Dylan pouted.

Prue laughed and leaned back in her chair.

Oh, he was enjoying this. The sisters were so different. Piper, sweet and caring. Prue, fiercely intelligent but a bit guarded, even sharp-tongued.

Regardless of their differences, though, both sisters had one thing in common: They were literally falling victim to his fatal charms.

Once he'd given Prue a dose of the same powder he'd given Piper, she'd be as uncontrollably smitten with him as her sister was. From there, it would be simple to divide and conquer.

The Charmed Ones were unbeatable only if they worked together, Dylan thought. Individually, they weren't as strong. In fact, they were vulnerable. It should be easy to strip their powers from them.

Step one was complete. Step two was to make sure that Prue swallowed his magic potion.

"You're sure I can't tempt you?" Dylan asked again. He leaned a little closer. His jacket fell open to reveal his form-fitting shirt. He had to be careful to hide his amusement when Prue's eyes darted to his broad chest underneath.

"Buckland's is right across the street from one of my favorite coffee bars," he coaxed.

"You don't mean Michelangelo's, do you?" Prue asked, her tone intrigued. "I go there all the time."

"Of course I mean Michelangelo's," Dylan said at once. "They have the best biscotti in town."

"All right, I give up. You talked me into it," Prue said, raising her hands in a gesture of surrender, "but I can only spare twenty minutes."

Dylan gave her a smile calculated to dazzle. He helped her put her jacket on, letting his hands linger on her shoulders.

"I'm sure that will be more than enough time for what I have in mind," he murmured softly.

CHAPTER 4

Everyone I talked to seemed absolutely certain that Ronald Galvez committed the murders," Phoebe said a little glumly.

It was late Thursday afternoon, the day after her interview with Dean Williams. Phoebe and Brett were sitting in the campus library. Phoebe had already scanned the newspaper reports of the murder on microfiche.

"I even spent the morning going through old police records," she told Brett.

"And?" he asked.

"Nada," she reported. "The records from the case were gone. Vanished. Completely disappeared."

"Weird," Brett observed.

"It was more than weird. It was almost as if someone didn't want people reading that report and finding out what really happened," Phoebe said.

"So—dead end," Brett summed it up.

"Thanks for the insight," Phoebe muttered, glancing at the school yearbooks from the fifties that were spread out on the table in front of her.

She was hoping that looking at pictures of Betty, Ronald, and Charlotte might help her get a better sense of who they were, feel more in touch with them.

So far, it hadn't done much good. That was probably because she hadn't actually been able to open a yearbook yet. Every time she tried to work, Brett interrupted her.

First he'd insisted that he and Phoebe work in a remote, back corner of the library. He'd claimed this was because they'd have fewer chances of being disturbed. But the truth, as Phoebe suspected, was that Brett wanted a place with no one around so that *he* wouldn't be disturbed when he made his big move on her. Now she eyed him warily as he moved his chair closer and closer to hers.

The guy wasn't under the illusion that he was being subtle, was he? Phoebe wondered as she pulled a random yearbook toward her. Nineteen fifty-seven—the year before the murder. The victims would have graduated in 1959. Phoebe hadn't been able to locate the yearbook for 1958—the doomed year, the year of the party—in the stacks, which puzzled her. Had it vanished along with the missing police files?

Quickly, Phoebe flipped through the yearbook pages until she located Ronald Galvez's junior class picture. She had to admit, he did look pretty tough, sort of like James Dean. Dark hair. Dark eyes. Expression more than a little defiant. Even so, Phoebe could feel her sympathies stir toward him. Nobody had wanted his relationship with Betty to last. He must have felt as though the whole world was against him.

Had it been? Phoebe wondered.

She remembered Betty's uncle, the chief of police, who'd given his officers the orders to shoot to kill. Hadn't there been anyone to champion Ronald Galvez?

There had been, she realized suddenly. But Ronald's chief supporter had also been chief victim, Betty Warren.

Abruptly, Phoebe closed the yearbook. She leaned back in her chair so that the front two legs came up off the tile floor.

"It just doesn't feel right," she said. "Dean Williams, Professor Hagin, locals who lived in the area at the time of the murder . . . they all tell exactly the same story. It's just too neat, too tidy. And the murders weren't like that. They were brutal and ugly. I think there's something about all this we haven't discovered yet."

Phoebe gave a start as she felt Brett's arm ease across her shoulders. His chair squeaked as he moved even closer.

If he tells me there are things about me he'd

like to discover, I'm going to do something ugly, Phoebe thought.

"I can think of lots more interesting things to discover, Phoebe," Brett breathed in her ear.

Not exactly what she'd been so hoping not to hear. But close enough. Phoebe shifted her weight forward. The front legs of her chair dropped down, hard. The right one landed square on the instep of Brett's left foot.

"Ow!" he cried, releasing his hold on Phoebe and quickly scooting backward.

"Did that hurt?" Phoebe asked, doing her best to sound concerned. "Brett, I'm so sorry. And I've been so selfish. I've been doing all the talking. Why don't you tell me how your research went? Did you turn up anything unusual? Has there been any evidence of ghost sightings?"

Brett mumbled something under his breath.

"What?" Phoebe asked, smiling sweetly. "I'm afraid I didn't catch that."

"I haven't done it yet," Brett admitted.

Phoebe's smile stayed fixed in place. "Let me see if I've got this straight," she said. "I spend all of this morning going through grimy old police files. I spend all of yesterday afternoon interviewing various citizens and faculty members about the murders, generally making them uncomfortable and in some cases actively pissing them off, and you're telling me you've done absolutely nothing?"

"All right," Brett said, his tone surly as he got

to his feet. "No need to rub it in. I'm going." He moved off, favoring his left foot, and disappeared around the end of one of the tall book stacks.

Phoebe made a face after him. She'd tried to be nice, but Brett just couldn't take the hint. That being the case, she felt no guilt about using somewhat extreme tactics.

Phoebe got to her feet and tiptoed to the end of the row of book stacks. She peered around the corner. Now that Brett had gone, Phoebe's corner of the library seemed completely deserted.

Excellent, she thought. In that case, the coast was clear to proceed to phase two.

Swiftly, Phoebe returned to her seat and removed a slip of paper from her shirt pocket. She smoothed it out on the table in front of her. The paper had an incantation from *The Book of Shadows* written on it.

Phoebe had hoped to have some information from Brett about possible ghost sightings before going on to phase two. But even without that info, she was determined to move forward.

Her every instinct was telling her there was more to the story of the murders than people were admitting.

Living people, that is. But what might the dead tell her?

It was a question that could be answered only one way—by summoning a ghost. To do that, all Phoebe had to do was to read the incantation on the paper before her.

She hadn't told Prue and Piper she was doing this. Using a powerful incantation to call up the dead was definitely a thing she'd have preferred to do with them. Any spell was stronger—and safer—when cast with the Power of Three.

But Phoebe had barely seen either of her sisters since their dinner together earlier that week. Their schedules just didn't seem to be meshing. If Phoebe was going to complete the extra credit assignment in time, she couldn't afford to wait. She'd have to use the incantation on her own—and face the consequences.

So just get on with it, she told herself. She was a big witch. She'd faced demons and warlocks. How much damage could an itty-bitty teenage ghost do after beings like those?

Phoebe studied the spell one more time. It would allow her to summon only one ghost, but hey, that was definitely a start. She closed her eyes, and began to chant.

Guardians of Time, pull back the curtain.
Let mysteries of the past be certain.
Past from present no longer divide.
Send a spirit to lead me inside.
The actors are gone, yet let me see.
As I will it, so must it be.

Expectantly, Phoebe opened her eyes and looked around.

She was still sitting in the present-day library.

There wasn't a ghost or even a wisp of mist in sight.

Fighting off disappointment, Phoebe checked the spell. Had she mixed up the words? Left something out?

No, she'd done it right the first time. So where was her ghost?

Maybe the incantation isn't specific enough, Phoebe thought as she read the words again. It *was* kind of vague, now that she thought about it. *The Book of Shadows* hadn't exactly had an incantation that would summon the three ghosts Phoebe wanted, so she'd had to make do with a more general spell. Maybe it wasn't enough to summon the spirits of Betty, Ronald, or Charlotte.

I'll check the book again tonight, Phoebe decided. If there was one thing she'd learned since becoming a witch, it was that things didn't always work out the way you planned.

She folded up the piece of paper containing the useless incantation and returned it to her shirt pocket. Perhaps tonight Piper or Prue would be around and they could help her.

Meantime, Phoebe reached to pull another of the yearbooks toward her. Her hand froze on the leather binding. From behind her came the sound of crying. It must be another student, Phoebe thought. Probably someone having your everyday garden-variety sobfest over a romantic breakup or a bad grade.

Maybe I'd better see if she's okay, Phoebe thought.

She got up, walked to the end of the stacks, and headed to her right, toward the sound of the crying. She stopped when she realized that the sound was fading. Had the girl stopped crying? No, she could still hear her. But now the sound seemed to be coming from her left.

Phoebe backtracked but the sound of the girl crying moved again. Phoebe could swear it was coming from the reading alcove near the maps. She walked over to the alcove and found it empty.

Phoebe felt the back of her neck begin to prickle. Was the girl who was crying moving around? Or had her incantation been successful after all? Was the eerie sound coming from a ghost?

Phoebe took a deep breath. There's nothing to be afraid of, she told herself as she moved through the stacks. This is the library, after all. There are other students and librarians in here—she swallowed hard—somewhere.

She reached the end of a set of shelves and peered around to the right, sure that was where the sound was coming from.

Nothing. Absolutely nothing, actually. As soon as Phoebe stuck her head around the stack, the crying stopped.

Had she just imagined all that sobbing? Phoebe massaged her temples. Maybe it was time she called it a day and went home. She started back toward the table where her things were. Then she heard the crying again.

This time it was louder—and directly behind her.

Heart pounding, Phoebe spun around.

This isn't really happening, she thought. She was absolutely, positively certain the sound of crying had come from just behind her.

So why wasn't anyone there?

Weird library acoustics, Phoebe told herself. Some trick that was the result of the sound bouncing off the tall book shelves. There was probably even a scientific name for it that Prue would know.

Yeah, right, Phoebe thought. Like the Halliwell Panic Attack Syndrome.

It was silly to be so freaked about a sound that could have so many perfectly logical explanations. She just hadn't figured out the right one yet.

Silently, Phoebe glided back the way she'd come. The sound grew louder as she paced back down the stacks.

Okay, this time I know I've got it right, she thought. She reached the opening in the stacks that led to her own table and walked past it.

The crying sound stopped once more. It was all Phoebe could do not to stomp her foot in frustration.

"Is someone there?" she called softly.

As if on cue, the crying began again, only this time it was everywhere. Phoebe was completely surrounded. The sobbing grew louder and louder. Phoebe controlled the urge to press her hands against her ears.

Stop it! she wanted to cry out. But her voice was gone, frozen with panic. Not only that, she was no longer alone. Phoebe's eyes were working just fine, even if her voice wasn't, and they were telling her that someone was in the stacks. Someone who was moving straight for her.

It was a young woman—a little younger than Phoebe. Phoebe tried to make out the details of her appearance. Then, with a jolt, she realized why she couldn't.

The young woman's body wasn't there. Or at least, not for more than a second at a time. It flickered in and out of view. Just the way a ghost's would, Phoebe thought.

Apparently, her incantation had worked.

The flickering figure approached Phoebe, then suddenly stopped, hovering at the end of the stack closest to her.

It's probably up to me to make the first move, Phoebe figured. I summoned her, after all. The trouble was, it was hard to make conversation when your voice was stuck in your throat.

Phoebe closed her eyes and sucked in a deep breath through her nose. It's just a ghost, she told herself, and I've got to communicate with her. I've got to find out what she knows.

Phoebe opened her eyes. The young woman was nowhere to be seen. In the next instant, Phoebe felt an icy chill pour over her. Had the ghost just swept right by?

Wait! she tried to call out. Please don't leave. I want to talk to you!

"Beware," a low voice moaned all around her. *"Beware!"*

Okay, that's it, Phoebe decided. It was time to bail. Now!

She tried to run but discovered the rest of her body was as frozen as her voice. She couldn't seem to move a muscle. She was stuck right where she was.

Before her startled eyes, books from the stacks all around her began flying through the air, slapping against the tiles as they hit the floor.

Phoebe could do absolutely nothing to protect herself. She couldn't move—couldn't even duck. She watched in horror as an entire row of books flew off the shelves, one after the other. Each one, moving closer and closer to her.

The bookcase right across from her gave an unearthly groan. Then it slowly began to tilt toward Phoebe, books sliding off its shelves.

Oh, no, she thought. No, no, no!

It was going to fall right on her!

CHAPTER 5

Phoebe watched in horror as the bookcase continued to topple toward her. She was going to be crushed! And there was absolutely nothing she could do about it.

Then, without warning, Phoebe felt herself shoot forward, almost as if she'd been pushed from behind. In the next instant, with a final groan, the heavy wooden bookcase crashed to the ground.

Phoebe didn't even want to think about what would have happened to her if she'd been beneath it. Phoebe pancake time.

On legs that trembled just a little more than she liked, Phoebe dashed to the table where she'd been working, snatched up her bag and jacket, then headed for the library door.

She could hear people yelling and the sound of running feet. The crashing of the bookcase had attracted the attention of the librarian, not to mention the other occupants of the library.

Phoebe felt a little guilty about leaving without explaining what had happened. But what could she say? I summoned a ghost, and it tried to kill me by knocking over a bookcase?

She didn't think so.

"Idiot," Phoebe mumbled to herself as she hit the push bar on the library door and sprinted down the front steps. "Lamebrain. Moron."

What had she been thinking, trying to summon a ghost by herself? She definitely should have waited until Prue and Piper could help her. After all, she was calling somebody back from the grave. Somebody who probably hadn't been very happy to be put there in the first place—and who apparently hadn't appreciated Phoebe's summons.

Phoebe located her car in the nearest parking lot and was fumbling for her keys when a blur of movement in the dusk light caught her eye. She started, and her keys dropped to the ground.

The ghost had followed her! It had found her!

Phoebe stood, heart thundering, her keys completely forgotten, and stared at the figure. After a moment, she realized the figure was moving *away* from her, not toward her, weaving back and forth between parked cars.

Quickly, she picked up her keys, unlocked the door, and slid into the driver's seat. She slammed the door shut, locked it, then sat for a moment to regain her composure.

Okay, maybe that wasn't a ghost. The last time Phoebe had had an incident with her car—the note on the windshield—she'd been pretty sure Wendy Chang was involved.

Phoebe drummed her fingers on the steering wheel, thinking hard. Could she be mistaken about what happened in the library, too? She'd been all primed to see a ghost since she'd just recited that incantation. But did that mean she'd actually seen one? Stress could do strange things to a person's mind.

Could Wendy have been responsible for the falling bookcase? Phoebe wondered suddenly. What if Wendy overheard Brett's clumsy attempt to make a pass? What if Wendy was escalating her campaign to make sure Phoebe stayed away from him? What if she was the one crying like that in the stacks?

All of a sudden, Phoebe realized her head was pounding.

Which was worse? she wondered. Being stalked or being haunted?

Definitely time to go home, she decided. She started the car and pulled out of the parking spot. She was halfway to the exit when she caught a glimpse of a figure in her peripheral vision, moving slowly but surely toward her through the parked cars—and about to walk directly in front of Phoebe's moving one.

Phoebe slowed down and tapped her horn. Probably just another student, worrying about an assignment or something, she thought. It was easy to get preoccupied. When the figure continued toward her, Phoebe hit the horn again.

Hellooo. Time to wake up and notice how much bigger the car is than you are, she thought.

The figure stepped straight into the path of Phoebe's car. Crying out in dismay, Phoebe lifted her foot from the gas pedal and stomped down on the brake, hard.

Time seemed to slow as the brakes squealed, and Phoebe was jerked forward against her seat belt. The figure stopped moving directly in front of Phoebe's car. Slowly, it turned to face her.

Oh, no, Phoebe thought. Oh, please, no!

It was a young woman, about the same age as the one Phoebe had seen in the library. But this girl wasn't flickering like a dying light bulb. She was all too real. The girl's face looked ghastly, her skin a strange and sickly gray. She was dressed in a pale pink party dress, fitted through the bodice and full through the skirt, like in pictures Phoebe had seen of Grace Kelly.

But it wasn't the cut of the dress that drew Phoebe's attention. It was what was on the dress. The entire front of it was covered in what looked exactly like bright red blood.

All of a sudden, Phoebe hurtled into action, throwing the car into park and flinging open the door. She hadn't hit this young woman, had she?

She hadn't felt any impact, but it was hard to know what was really happening in crisis situations.

Phoebe dashed toward the front of the car.

By the time she reached it, no one was there. The girl was gone.

Phoebe knelt and examined the front of her car. Bumper, headlights, and hood—they could definitely use a wash, but that was only because of the usual city grime. There was no blood on the car.

Her heartbeat returning to normal, Phoebe got back into her vehicle. Okay, so she hadn't hit anyone. This was good. But she was also certain that she hadn't imagined the girl in the blood-soaked dress.

I've got to get home, she thought. I have to talk to Prue and Piper.

Now Phoebe was sure that her incantation had worked. She really had summoned somebody back from the dead, which might not have been one of her better ideas.

In fact, Phoebe admitted to herself as she drove home, she was beginning to have a very, *very* bad feeling about it.

At Halliwell Manor Prue carried a fresh bunch of daisies in from the kitchen, where she'd been arranging them in a vase. She set the vase on the living room coffee table, then stood back to admire her handiwork.

Pretty good, she thought. Best of all, there was

no need to pick these flowers apart to tell the future of her love life. Things were going absolutely fine.

Actually, they were more than fine, Prue thought as she settled on the couch and opened the novel she was reading. Since meeting Dylan—had it really been only a couple of days ago?—Prue's whole outlook on love had changed. She'd never felt so strongly about a guy, or so certain that things would go well.

She hadn't had a chance to tell Piper or Phoebe about him yet, so today she had deliberately come home early, hoping to catch her sisters. They were due to arrive at any moment.

Prue heard a car pull up and a car door slam. She bounded up from the couch, her book forgotten. One of her sisters was home, at least. Now she could share her amazing news.

By the time she reached the door, she'd heard a second car pull up. Excellent! Now she could tell both of her sisters the good news together.

"Finally!" Prue said as she flung the front door open. A startled Phoebe stood on the other side. Piper was right behind her. "I thought you guys would never get here."

Phoebe stared at Piper. "Are we late for something?"

"Who cares?" Piper answered, sounding ridiculously happy. "You guys, I have the most amazing news."

"Can it wait?" Phoebe interrupted as she barreled through the door. "I need help. We have to talk."

"But I need to tell you both *my* news," Prue said as Phoebe and Piper trooped by her. She trailed them into the living room, all three sisters talking at once.

"Okay, wait a minute. Hold everything!" Prue shouted. "Obviously, we all have important news to share," she went on in a quieter voice. "If we don't take turns, we'll never get it out. We should just go one at a time. Since I'm the oldest, I get to go first."

Phoebe rolled her eyes. "I knew this was going to end up with me being last," she muttered. Grabbing Piper by the arm, she steered her over to the couch. She urged her down, then sat beside her, clasping her hands in her lap like a well-behaved schoolchild.

"All right, Miss Halliwell. We're ready now," she said. "Though I still think my news should go first since it's the most important."

"Nothing can be more important than my news," Prue insisted. She paused for extra effect. "I've met the most fabulous guy, and I think I'm in love!"

"That's so great!" Phoebe said at once. Then a look of confusion crossed her face. "Wait a minute," she went on. "When did all this happen?"

Prue opened her mouth to speak, but Piper interrupted her. "But that's just what *I* was going to say!" she exclaimed. "I'm in love, too! Is that incredible timing or what?"

"Okay, now you both really have to slow down," Phoebe said. "Two sisters in love at exactly the same time? You two haven't, by any chance, been experimenting with love potions?"

"Of course not," Prue said at once. "We can't use the spells in *The Book of Shadows* for our own personal gain, Phoebe. You know that as well as I do."

"Okay, so spill," Phoebe directed. "I want the usual stuff first. Who? How? When? Where?"

"At one of the morning auctions at Buckland's," Prue responded, answering the last question first. "I think it was just the beginning of this week, though it seems like we've known each other practically forever. I've never felt so close to a guy so fast. It's absolutely amazing!"

"I know just what you mean," Piper put in. "I feel just the same way about Dylan."

Prue's mouth dropped open. She could feel a potent heat pounding through her veins.

"What did you just say?" she asked Piper.

"That's exactly how I feel about the guy I've met," Piper explained. "His name is Dylan—Dylan Thomas. His band, Dylan and the Good Nights, is playing at the club. Isn't that just the most clever name for the band? I thought Dylan's name was a joke at first, until he explained that his mother—"

"—was an English major who spent her honeymoon in Wales," Prue finished for her.

"Uh-oh," Phoebe muttered under her breath. "Trouble."

"That's right," Piper said, her tone plainly puzzled. "But how did you know about Dylan's mother?"

"Because *I'm* the one in love with Dylan!" Prue all but shouted.

"Okay, time out," Phoebe said, swiftly rising to her feet. "You both got to tell your news, now I get to tell mine. Then you can decide who saw Dreamboat first. I'll even ring the bell for the first round."

Prue felt another wave of heat pulse through her. This could be the most important relationship of her life, and Phoebe was making jokes about it!

"I don't appreciate that remark, Phoebe," she said stiffly. "After all the support I've given you over the years, the least you could do is support me now."

"Hey, wait a minute," Piper protested. "I've given her just as much support as you have."

"No, you haven't," Prue came right back. "I'm the oldest."

"What does that have to do with anything?" Piper queried, shooting to her feet. "All you're doing now is trying to change the subject. But it won't work. The fact is I saw Dylan first."

Phoebe collapsed back onto the couch and put her head in her hands. "Guys, really, I do *not* need this right now."

"*When* did you see him first?" Prue demanded as she faced off with Piper. She could feel the blood racing through her veins. It felt like it was boiling.

What is going on with me? Prue wondered through the haze of her anger. I can't ever remember being so mad at Piper. Maybe I should try to calm down, think about this logically.

But every time Prue thought of Dylan and Piper together—she simply couldn't stand it. There was no way that she could approach this situation logically.

It's just a sign of how important my relationship with Dylan is to me, she decided. Proof positive that he's *my* Mr. Right. No rival was going to take Dylan away from her, even if that rival happened to be Piper.

"I met Dylan at the club." Piper was enunciating each word very clearly. "On Tuesday afternoon."

"Too late!" Prue declared triumphantly. "*I* met him at the auction Tuesday morning."

"Well, okay, but I *talked* to him first," Piper pointed out. "He called me the week before, to book Dylan and the Good Nights into the club. That means I had first contact."

"Doesn't count," Prue said at once. "I *saw* him first."

"It does so count," Piper shot back.

"Will you two please stop it?" Phoebe shouted. "Just stop it!"

A startled pause filled the Halliwell living room.

"Honestly," Phoebe went on. "Just chill out and listen to yourselves. You don't sound like two grown women discussing a relationship. You sound like five-year-olds arguing over a toy on Christmas morning."

"As if," Prue scoffed.

"Yeah, right," Piper snorted.

"STOP IT RIGHT NOW!" Phoebe shouted. "What is wrong with you two? I'm in a situation where I really need your help. Both of you are just going to have to put your personal relationships aside for a moment."

Prue regarded Piper for a moment. "I can if you can," she finally challenged.

"I can do anything you can do," Piper promised.

"Okay, fine," Phoebe put in, before any further argument could develop. She took Prue by the shoulders and sat her on one end of the couch, then positioned Piper on the other.

"Now, just sit still and listen for a minute," she said.

Quickly, Phoebe outlined her school project and what had happened that day in the library and the parking lot.

"What were you thinking?" Prue asked when she was finished. "You tried to summon the dead without even consulting us? You know that's not the kind of magic you call up casually."

Piper nodded. "I hate to say this, Phoebe, but that is so like you."

"I *wasn't* being casual. And I've already admitted that I made a mistake, trying it on my own," Phoebe said, her tone sharp. "It's why I'm coming to you *now* and asking for your *help*."

"Okay," Prue said. "What do you want us to do?"

"I think we should cast a counterspell to protect me from whoever or whatever it is I've summoned," Phoebe told her. "Send it back to wherever it came from. Then I want us to work together to solve these Halloween Murders. I'm sure there's more to them than meets the eye."

"All right," Prue said, rising to her feet. "Let's get this over with."

"Gee, Prue," Phoebe said sarcastically. "Thanks so much for your enthusiastic support."

"Hey," Prue said, growing angry again, with Phoebe this time. "I'm not the one who screwed up."

"Oh, come on, Prue. Cut her some slack," Piper put in.

Prue pointed a finger at Piper. "Don't think you can fool me," she said. "I know what you're doing. You're going to disagree with everything I say, just because you *know* I was the first one to see Dylan."

"Oh, grow up!" Piper snapped. "It doesn't matter that you saw him first."

It does, too, Prue thought furiously, but decided she would no longer stoop to Piper's level of immaturity. "I'm going upstairs to check *The Book of Shadows* for a counterincantation," she said in a cool, dignified tone. "*I* want to *help* Phoebe. She should be able to depend on at least one of her sisters."

Piper shot to her feet, her expression totally outraged. "What was that remark supposed to mean?"

"If you can't figure it out, I'm certainly not going to tell you," Prue said, unable to keep the satisfaction from her voice.

With that parting remark, Prue turned and walked up the stairs. All the way up to the attic, she felt sure Dylan was with her, approving of her actions.

When it came to love, it was every witch for herself.

But with every step she took, Prue wondered why, instead of seeing Dylan's face as she'd done before, this time she could have sworn she heard the sound of his laughter.

"Okay," Phoebe said fifteen minutes later. She was staring at a page in *The Book of Shadows* filled with cramped, spidery handwriting. "This isn't exactly a counterincantation, but it is supposed to banish 'phantasms.' It looks like it will work. The only problem is we need to get some ingredients together before we can cast the spell."

"What kind of ingredients?" Prue asked. She was staring out the attic window, on the opposite side of the room from Piper.

Phoebe winced. " 'Earth from a widower's grave, gathered beneath a full moon,' " she read aloud.

"Gross," Piper said. "Besides, last night was full moon. You're going to have to wait two weeks."

"I don't think I have two weeks," Phoebe said nervously. "Maybe we can improvise on the moon part. There's something else we'd need. 'A token from one who romances the heart.' "

"*That* is not a problem," Prue declared airily. "I already have a token from Dylan."

"What token?" Piper demanded.

Prue's ice blue eyes took on a dangerous gleam. "He wrote me a note, asking me out."

"Oh, I'd love to see that," Piper scoffed.

"I wouldn't!" Phoebe shouted. She rubbed her forehead and tried to calm herself. "Look, are you two going to help me—or are you going to fight over some guy?"

"I'm going to get Dylan's note," Prue said, starting out of the attic.

"And *if* she's actually got one," Piper muttered, following after her, "I'm going to shred it."

"Oh, thank you, both," Phoebe said. "That was very helpful."

She watched her sisters go, a look of astonishment on her face. What was going on in this house? And how was she ever going to deal with the ghost who was haunting her?

* * *

Late that night Phoebe sat in one of the campus study halls, working on her extra-credit project. She hadn't really planned on a late-night session away from home, but staying at Halliwell Manor and listening to Prue and Piper's constant bickering had finally just been too much for her.

Phoebe still couldn't figure out quite why her sisters were behaving the way they were. Could any guy really be that great? That important?

"Hey, Phoebe."

Phoebe glanced up. Brett Weir stood beside her. Great. More potential guy trouble. But maybe Brett had learned his lesson after the episode in the library earlier that day. He was looking hesitant.

"Hi," she said, deciding to take pity on him.

"Decided to study late, huh?" Brett asked.

"Seemed like the thing to do," she said. "Want to join me?"

Instantly, Brett's expression brightened. He pulled out the chair beside hers and sat down. "I'm kind of surprised to see you here," he confided.

"Why?" Phoebe asked.

Brett maneuvered his chair a little closer, and Phoebe could hear the beginnings of the warning bells clanging in the back of her mind. Was this déjà vu or what?

"Well, you know," Brett said. "Good-looking woman like you, I figured you probably had a date or something."

Right, every night of the week, Phoebe thought. *What was wrong with this guy?* she wondered. *Could he just not take a hint?* He was either incredibly persistent or incredibly dumb.

Plainly, Phoebe was going to have to resort to more desperate measures.

"As a matter of fact," she fibbed, "I am seeing someone."

This information didn't appear to deter Brett in the least. He scooted a little closer.

Okay, that's it! Phoebe thought. Abruptly, she rose to her feet and began to put her study materials away, making no effort to control or hide her irritation. The entire evening had been a disaster from start to finish. Brett Weir definitely was not helping.

To Phoebe's dismay, Brett rose, too. He pushed her chair out of the way and stepped in close, leaving Phoebe nowhere to go. She was trapped between Brett and the study table. She could feel the edge of it digging into the backs of her thighs.

"I'll bet I can make you forget about the guy you're seeing," Brett murmured. "I'd really like to do that, Phoebe."

You are so deluded, Phoebe thought.

Brett took another step. Now he was pressed against her. Phoebe felt a tiny spurt of fear mingle with her irritation.

This was beyond annoying. It was coming close to harassment.

"I really don't want to hurt you, Brett," she said. "But if you don't step back right now—"

Brett gave a throaty laugh and put his arms around her.

"Oh, come on, Phoebe," he said. "You don't have to pretend to resist. You don't really want to fight me. Girls like a guy who takes control. Wendy certainly did."

Yeah, right, Phoebe thought. Look where it got her.

"Control this," she said aloud. And brought one knee up. Hard.

Some change in her expression must have finally caught Brett's attention. At the last second, he jerked back, out of range. Phoebe's knee connected with the inside of his leg instead of the more sensitive part of his anatomy that had been her target.

Brett's face darkened. "What did you do that for?" he asked in a tight, angry voice. "All I wanted was one little kiss."

"Well, maybe you should have asked for one instead of just trying to take it," Phoebe said, her tone a match for his. To think she'd actually felt sorry for him!

If her sisters' luck with men was anything like hers, she really ought to go right home and tell them to dump Mr. Right. He was probably a warlock or something.

"I'm only going to say this one more time, Brett," Phoebe said. "Try to pay attention because the basic concept seems to be hard for you to grasp." She stepped toward him, jabbing her finger against his chest to accentuate her words. "I—am—not—interested. If you can't deal with that, get yourself another project and another partner."

Brett brushed by her roughly and stalked off, leaving her alone in the study hall. Phoebe plopped back down in her chair and put her head in her hands.

What was wrong with the world today? she wondered. Was some sort of strange and unnatural cosmic convergence occurring that she hadn't noticed in her star chart?

This day had been one of the worst and weirdest Phoebe could recall, and she had to admit, she'd known some. The only good thing that could be said for it was that it was almost over. Phoebe figured not much more could happen. It was late. Time to go home.

She lifted her head from her hands and felt her breath catch at the base of her throat.

Hovering in the air in front of her was a young woman in a pale pink party dress. The front of the dress was covered in blood.

Phoebe knew she was in the presence of one of the ghosts of the Halloween murders.

CHAPTER 6

The specter hovered in the air before Phoebe, the pale pink of her dress contrasting harshly with the bright red blood that spattered it.

Phoebe thought she saw the young woman's lips move, as though she was attempting to speak. But if she was, Phoebe couldn't hear her. She couldn't hear anything over the frantic ringing in her ears. Phoebe felt sheer terror stiffening every muscle in her body. Was she about to be totally paralyzed again, the way she'd been in the library?

Then, without warning, the ghost drifted lower until it seemed to Phoebe that she was sitting on the floor. Her bloody pink skirts spread out around her, the young woman put her head in her hands. Phoebe could see her shoulders shake, as if she was sobbing uncontrollably. At this sight, Phoebe felt some of her paralyzing fear begin to drain away.

The ghost didn't want to hurt her, she realized. Instead, this young woman was herself in terrible pain.

Maybe I can help her, Phoebe thought. Maybe that's why she keeps appearing to me.

If only the two of them could speak to each other!

Phoebe cleared her throat, experimentally. Sound came out. Vocal cords working. So far, so good.

"Who are you?" she asked. Her voice sounded shaky and funny, even to her own ears.

At the sound of Phoebe's voice, the ghost girl lifted her head. Phoebe saw the girl's lips part and felt her own heartbeat accelerate in anticipation.

"Char-Charlotte," the girl in pink said. Her voice sounded weak—as if it took immense effort for her to speak.

"Charlotte Logan? Betty Warren's best friend?" Phoebe asked. The girl nodded her head. "Can you—do you want to tell me something?" Phoebe asked.

Again Charlotte Logan nodded her head.

Phoebe thought her heart was going to explode through her chest, it was pounding so hard. The truth about the Halloween Murders might be seconds away.

"What?" Phoebe asked. "Do you want to tell

me what really happened the night you were killed?"

Charlotte's face seemed to crumple, as if she were being overcome by uncontrollable grief.

"Betty," she sobbed, her face in her hands.

"What about Betty?" Phoebe pressed.

"She was my friend."

"I know," Phoebe said. "She was your best friend, right?"

The ghost's shoulders heaved with another sob.

"But you didn't like Ronald Galvez?"

The ghost looked up, her eyes tear-streaked. "I never wanted things to end the way they did," she said, her voice trembling.

"I believe that." The last of Phoebe's fear vanished as she felt her heart go out to Charlotte. The ghost was being torn apart by grief and probably had been for the last forty years.

"Will you tell me what happened that night?" Phoebe asked. "Did Ronald Galvez really commit the murders? Did he kill you and Betty?"

Charlotte dropped her head into her hands again. "No."

"No?" Phoebe felt her pulse jump with excitement. Her intuition was right. Ronald Galvez was innocent! But she needed proof. "Charlotte," she said carefully. "If Ronald wasn't the killer, then who was?"

The ghost lifted her head and rubbed at a bloodstain on her dress. For a long moment she seemed totally absorbed in this. At last she said, "The man in the mask."

"What man in what mask?"

"I don't know." The ghost sounded weak, forlorn.

"But there was someone else in that room besides you and Betty and Ronald?"

"You have the power. You have to see," Charlotte answered, then her body seemed to grow transparent and began to flicker, as if she were out of energy.

"Charlotte, wait," Phoebe pleaded. "You haven't told me—"

But the ghost was gone.

Phoebe slumped back in her chair, exhausted and more confused than ever. Who was the man in the mask? she asked herself. Considering that the murders took place at a Halloween party, there could have been lots of guys in masks. That really didn't narrow things down a whole lot.

And what was that last thing Charlotte said, about Phoebe having to see? Am I supposed to have another vision? Phoebe wondered.

Only one thing was actually clear. Ronald Galvez did not kill Betty and Charlotte—someone else did. And it was up to Phoebe to find out who. If there was a chance that she could uncover the truth of the Halloween murders, Phoebe knew she had to take it. Especially if it helped her get a killer grade in the process.

* * *

I'm going to go through with this, Piper decided. I want to make things right.

It was about ten-thirty the following morning, the time Piper knew Prue usually stepped out of her office for some coffee. Piper was in her car on the way to Buckland's. Between dreaming of Dylan and worrying about her argument with Prue, Piper hadn't gotten much sleep the night before. As a result, she really couldn't claim she was at her best this morning.

Regardless of that, however, Piper had come to an important decision over her second cup of morning coffee. She was going to apologize to Prue for the way she'd behaved last night. In the clear morning light of a new day, Piper couldn't quite believe she and her older sister had argued so vehemently over a guy they'd both only just met. It simply wasn't like them.

I guess the fact that I'm interested in Dylan, too, just struck a raw nerve with Prue, Piper decided as she circled the block, searching for a parking place. Especially since it wasn't long after Prue had been shredding daisies, trying to peer into the future of her love life that all this happened, she remembered.

Piper hit her turn signal and carefully backed her car into a spot.

It should have been apparent to a total idiot that Prue was feeling in need of support. Had Piper given her any? She didn't think so. If anything, she'd done just the opposite. She'd staked a claim for herself and refused to let go. Honestly, she and Prue had argued over Dylan like children who both wanted to play with the same toy. If that wasn't degrading to both parties, Piper didn't know what was.

By the time she entered the Buckland's lobby, Piper was smiling, confident that she and Prue would both have a good laugh over how strangely they'd behaved.

First, though, Piper planned to tell Prue she was sorry for the way she'd acted. Prue would apologize, too. Then they'd treat each other to a mocha. Whole milk. With whip.

After that, Piper reminded herself as she breezed through Prue's door with a quick knock, they'd better find out what was bugging Phoebe.

"Piper!"

Prue was seated behind her desk, an enormous stack of papers in front of her. It was so tall, Piper could barely see Prue's eyes peering at her over the top.

"Good grief!" Piper exclaimed.

Prue rolled her eyes. "Tell me about it. It's the paperwork for this auction that's supposed to happen early next month. It will take practically every second I have between now and then to get it ready."

"Then I won't take long," Piper promised. "Really, Prue, the only reason I came by was to talk about last night."

Above the stack of papers, Prue's eyes grew

a little wary. "What about last night?" she asked.

"You know—about Dylan." Piper stopped. Why was this so hard all of a sudden? Driving over, she'd been perfectly sure of what she'd wanted to do. But at the mention of Dylan's name, Piper felt her whole body flush with heat. Suddenly she was angry with Prue all over again.

Why should I be the one to apologize? Piper asked herself. After all, I was the one who was in touch with Dylan first. That gives me first rights, no matter what Prue says.

If anyone should apologize for her behavior, it was Prue. She was trying to cut Piper out, sabotage the chance for her perfect romance!

"What about Dylan?" Prue asked, her tone definitely wary now.

Piper felt her body heat shoot up a notch. She couldn't stand to hear Prue so much as mention Dylan's name. In a rush of heated anger, Piper strode to Prue's desk and shoved the stack of papers onto the floor.

"Stay away from him," she said menacingly. "I mean it, Prue. He's mine. If you know what's good for you, stay out of my way."

Prue rose to her feet, her blue eyes glittering. "Don't think you can scare me, Piper—and don't think for a minute I'm going to back off. Dylan is *my* Mr. Right, and I can prove it."

"Oh, sure," Piper scoffed. But even through the heat of her anger, she felt a cold fear clutch her heart. Prue couldn't really prove Dylan was hers, could she? That note Dylan had written didn't prove a thing.

Piper crossed her arms and glared at her sister. "You're just trying to scare me off."

Prue leaned back, a satisfied expression on her face. "And it's working, isn't it?" she asked sweetly.

Piper had a sudden impulse to throw something—preferably Prue—out the nearest window.

"Okay, how?" she challenged. "How will you prove Dylan wants you more than me?"

"He's asked me to the concert Saturday night," Prue said, her tone triumphant.

Piper felt her stomach plummet. "Tomorrow night? That's *my* concert," she protested. "The one at P3."

An expression Piper could only describe as smug crossed Prue's face. "Precisely. And he didn't invite you to go with him. He invited me."

"He doesn't need to invite me, Prue," Piper informed her sister in a lofty tone. "It's at my club."

Prue's expression grew impatient. "It doesn't make any difference!" she exclaimed. "On Saturday night you, Dylan, and I will all be in the same place at the same time. He'll have to choose between us. And you'd just better get ready for the fact that he's going to choose me."

"You are so conceited and so wrong," Piper said in a pitying tone. "I really feel sorry for you, Prue. You're not going to be able to cope when

Dylan chooses me." With that, she marched to the door, her head held high.

But Piper's stomach was churning. She hated that the three of them would be forced to face one another in public, in the middle of her club. Still, she knew she couldn't afford to let Prue see she felt that way. That would be caving.

"I hope you like crow, Prue," she said, one hand on the doorknob. "Because you're going to be eating a lot of it on Saturday. I'll have my chef prepare a special sauce just for you."

"Stuff it, Piper," Prue said.

Piper smiled. "Whatever you say."

Then she waltzed out the door before Prue could get another word in.

Well, Piper thought as she made her way back to her car. That hadn't gone quite the way she'd planned, but at least she'd gotten the last word. And where Prue was concerned, that didn't happen very often.

Not only that, there was still time between now and Saturday, Piper realized suddenly. Time she could use to good advantage if she played her cards right. After all, Dylan and the Good Nights still had tonight's practice session at P3. That would throw Piper and Dylan together.

Piper smiled as she fed a handful of quarters into the parking meter. It was time to stack the deck in her favor a bit, she decided. If it was true that all was fair in love and war, it was also true that nothing spiked the enemy's guns like an effective bout of shopping.

Piper set off in the direction of her favorite boutique, which happened to be conveniently located around the corner from Buckland's.

If Prue thought Piper would wimp out just because she was usually the nice sister, then she was sorely mistaken.

Phoebe poured herself a bowl of cereal and sleepily eyed the morning paper. She'd slept in late today, but she figured she deserved it after her ghost encounter the night before.

Her eyes opened a little wider as she skimmed the headline near the bottom of the front page: "Halloween Hauntings Early This Year? Rumors of Ghosts at Community College."

"Ghosts?" Phoebe murmured to herself. "As in Charlotte, Betty, and Ronald?"

"It's truth, not rumor. We were there last night. In Thayer Hall."

Phoebe nearly dropped her bowl of cereal as she realized that the bloodied ghost of Charlotte Logan was sitting at her kitchen table.

"Have you seen?" the ghost asked her.

"Seen what?" Phoebe replied, trying not to sound as spooked as she felt. She just wasn't prepared for being cross-examined by a ghost before breakfast.

"What happened that night," Charlotte answered.

Phoebe sat down at the table but pushed her

cereal away. The sight of Charlotte's blood-spattered dress kind of ruined her appetite.

"I think I'd better explain," Phoebe said. "Sometimes I get glimpses of the past. But these visions just kind of happen. I can't predict when I'll get one or what I'll see—and I haven't had a vision since I saw you last night."

The ghost gazed at the kitchen table, giving Phoebe the distinct feeling that she was disappointed in her.

"Let me ask you a question," Phoebe said. "Who was the man in the mask?"

The ghost covered her face with her hands and began to sob.

"He killed Betty, right?" Phoebe probed.

Charlotte nodded. Or maybe her shoulders just heaved? Phoebe wasn't sure.

"And you?"

The ghost nodded again.

"What about Ronald? He wasn't the masked man, was he?"

Charlotte raised her head, her eyes clear. "No."

"So there *was* a fourth person in that back room," Phoebe said carefully. "Someone who stabbed Betty, then you. How did Ronald wind up with the knife?"

"He fought," Charlotte answered. "To save us."

The pieces were finally falling into place. Phoebe couldn't keep the excitement out of her voice. "So Ronald told the truth. And all these years his spirit has been restless, trying to get someone else to believe him and clear his name."

"We must all return," the ghost said.

"You mean, all three ghosts are bound to return and haunt the campus?"

"You must help us—until the truth is known," Charlotte said.

"How?" Phoebe asked. "What do you want me to do?"

"The anniversary of our deaths," the ghost said haltingly. "As it was, it must be again."

Phoebe felt the muscles in her chest tighten with fear. "It must be again?" she echoed. "Excuse me, but that night in 1958 was a disaster. I'm not really eager to see any of that repeated."

"You must go inside!"

"Inside what? Thayer Hall?"

"No!" Now Charlotte looked positively distressed, and Phoebe could feel her own frustration mounting. If the ghost was so eager to communicate with her, why couldn't they have a normal conversation? Why did it have to be so hard for her to talk?

"You must go inside," the ghost insisted.

This time the hairs on the back of Phoebe's neck rose as she realized there was another meaning for that phrase. Hadn't that been exactly what she asked for when she cast the first spell—a spirit "to lead her inside"?

Phoebe summoned her courage. "Tell me how," she asked. "Please!"

"That night. It must be again and you must see. You must tell the truth. Then we will no longer have to return."

Phoebe rubbed her eyes, trying to make sense of this. Maybe what the ghost was asking for wasn't that impossible. After all, there was going to be a fifties Halloween party on Sunday night. They'd be playing the same kind of music. From what she'd heard, they were even trying to recreate the decor of the original party. The scene had already been set. It was pure coincidence, she realized, but maybe she should take advantage of it. Maybe this re-creation of that night was really what was meant to be.

"Let me see if I've got this straight," Phoebe said. "On Halloween night we re-create the party where you and Betty were killed, and Ronald wound up holding a bloody knife. And then?"

Charlotte's expression was nearly serene as she said, "It will all be again—on the spirit plane. You will see it happen just as you see me now. Then you will tell the truth about that night—and we will be able to rest in peace."

"So on Halloween night we'll restage the scene of the crimes, I'll go inside, or to the ghost plane," Phoebe said, thinking it through aloud. "And I'll see what really happened all those years ago, make the real story known, and then your spirits will finally rest in peace."

But if that was really the plan, she'd never be sure. Because Charlotte Logan's ghost had disappeared.

* * *

Later that afternoon, in the campus cafeteria, Phoebe regarded her fruit smoothie somberly. Ever since her breakfast chat with Charlotte's ghost, Phoebe had been wondering what to do.

She was pretty sure she was going to do exactly what Charlotte's ghost suggested: go to the party, let the reenactment occur, and witness what was happening among the ghosts so she could finally clear Ronald Galvez's name.

Still, this was not a risk-free plan. Phoebe had been practicing witchcraft long enough to know that events on the spirit plane often affected the everyday human plane—in a big way.

What if the murders were reenacted and real people died?

Not possible, Phoebe told herself. That wouldn't help the three ghosts rest. If anything, that would make things worse for them. Still, she'd feel a lot better if her sisters agreed to come to the party. That is, *if* she could get them to agree to anything.

Phoebe put her head down on her hands with a frustrated groan.

"Phoebe." An agitated voice had Phoebe raising her head swiftly. Her eyes met those of Marjorie Yarnell. Marjorie was standing beside Phoebe's table, clutching one of the flyers for the Halloween party.

"Have you seen this?" Marjorie asked.

Phoebe nodded. "Of course. They've been posted all over campus."

Marjorie sat down at the table, across from Phoebe. Nervously, she began to rearrange the packets of sweeteners in their metal holder. "I—I don't think it's a good idea," she began. "To have a party in the same place on the same date." Her green eyes met Phoebe's. "Please tell me you're not going to the party."

"Actually, I am," Phoebe told her. "Before I came here, I even signed up for decorating committee."

Since Charlotte had urged her to "see," Phoebe figured that setting up Thayer Hall the night before the party might be one route to a vision.

Marjorie's eyes were wide with disbelief. "What did you just say?"

"On Saturday night I'm going to help decorate for the party." Phoebe looked at Marjorie more closely. She was as carefully dressed and made-up as ever, but beneath her fine layer of blush Phoebe could see that her skin was deathly pale. "What's wrong, Marjorie?" she asked. "Why are you so worried about the party?"

"I just don't think it's a good idea to hold another costume party in what used to be Thayer Hall," Marjorie said, her fingers plucking nervously at the edge of the flyer. "It's just too gruesome somehow. And too unpredictable. Anything could happen."

You got that right, Phoebe thought. She could hardly tell Marjorie about her talk with Charlotte, however. Not without also revealing what she, herself, truly was. She didn't think Marjorie would be able to handle knowing that Phoebe was a witch.

"This isn't 1958," Phoebe gently reminded the older woman. "The events of the past can't really repeat themselves."

Now, if only I could convince myself of that, Phoebe thought.

"Oh, you're right. I'm sure you're probably right," Marjorie said, her voice unnaturally high. "But what about things like—oh, what do they call them—copycat crimes?"

Phoebe shrugged. "I guess that's always a possibility," she admitted. "But probably not too likely."

"What if that Galvez boy wasn't the murderer?" Marjorie went on. "What if the real culprit is still alive? He could even be here on campus! You know what they say—the guilty always revisit the scene of the crime."

Without warning, an image of Dean Williams popped into Phoebe's head. She remembered his voice as he'd assured her that Ronald Galvez was guilty of the murders.

"You can take my word for it," the dean had said.

Had Dean Williams been lying? Phoebe wondered. Trying to frighten her off before she could uncover evidence of his own guilt? Was it possible he was the one in the Halloween mask?

Phoebe shuddered as she realized that

Marjorie might be right. If the murderer was still alive and nearby, he'd probably be drawn to the re-enactment of that night.

Marjorie gave Phoebe an apologetic smile. "I'm afraid my imagination is getting the best of me again. I saw a police show on TV last night with a plot just like that."

"Oh," Phoebe said, feeling a little—but only a little—relieved.

"Actually," Marjorie went on, "I came to give you this." She reached down into the leather book bag she'd set beside the table. "It might help you with your extra-credit project. I was doing some research for another class and I found it in the basement of the library."

Phoebe's heartbeat accelerated when she saw what Marjorie was sliding across the table toward her. It was the yearbook for 1958, the year Betty, Ronald, and Charlotte went to the party. It was the one yearbook Phoebe had been unable to find.

"This is great!" Phoebe exclaimed, her excitement momentarily wiping out her fears.

Marjorie gave her a strange smile. "I'll leave you to it, then," she said. She stood, then hesitated for a moment. "There's a picture of Betty and Ronald on page forty-nine."

She spun on her heel and walked swiftly away from the table before Phoebe could reply.

Her pulse pounding as if she'd just run a race, Phoebe opened the yearbook. There'd been class photos of Ronald and Betty in the other yearbooks Phoebe had looked at. But nothing that showed the two of them together. Nothing that gave her any insight into the true nature of their relationship.

When Phoebe located page forty-nine she caught her breath. It was a page of candid photos. "Snapshots of Campus Life," read the headline across the top.

It was perfect, Phoebe thought. Exactly the sort of clue that she'd been looking for.

There was a picture of the football team, trying to build a human pyramid and toppling over. A shot of the yearbook office with the staff slumped over their typewriters. Another of the cheerleading squad hosting a bake sale.

And in the lower right-hand corner, a black-and-white photo of a group of seniors, smiling triumphantly for the camera. In the center, their arms around each other's waists, were Betty Warren and Ronald Galvez.

Instantly, Phoebe felt the jolt that meant a vision was beginning. For a moment the photograph in the yearbook seemed to recede into the distance. Then Phoebe could see Betty and Ronald, clasped tightly in each other's arms. They were in a room decorated with black crepe paper and jack-o'-lanterns. Betty wore a long dress. A tiara sparkled in her blond hair. Ronald was dressed as a pirate, wearing a gold hoop in one ear. He was totally gorgeous, Phoebe realized. They were dancing. Phoebe could hear the strains of Buddy Holly's "It's So Easy to Fall in Love" playing in the background.

Betty's face was radiant as she looked up at Ronald. It was easy to see that she was completely in love. Ronald's lips curved upward in a smile as he stared down at Betty. The Buddy Holly song ended, and "Earth Angel" began to play. Ronald bent his head and whispered something in Betty's ear. Betty blushed, and nodded, and the two moved off together. As they made their way through the crowd of other dancers, Phoebe lost them. She came back to reality with a lurch.

Long after her vision had ended, Phoebe sat perfectly still at her table, staring down at the picture of Betty and Ronald.

In Phoebe's vision, Ronald Galvez had acted the same way he had in this old photograph—like a young man who was deeply in love, not like a rebel without a cause. And certainly not like the desperate murderer he was later made out to be.

Who really did commit the murders? Phoebe wondered. Marjorie's suggestion that the real murderer might still be alive—and ready to revisit the scene of his crime—kept nagging at her.

Prue and Piper are going to have to help me, Phoebe decided. This was a job for the Power of Three if ever there was one. Because although

Phoebe was pretty sure she could handle the witnessing part by herself, there was one part of Halloween night she knew she couldn't handle on her own.

There was no way she could watch her own back.

CHAPTER 7

"Come on, you guys," Phoebe said later that afternoon. "You don't have to kiss and make up. I just want you to do this spell with me. It could be really important. I need the Power of Three."

From her position on the far side of the attic Prue shot Piper a glare. "You know I'm always ready to help you, Phoebe."

"Oh, and I suppose that's supposed to mean I'm not," Piper shot back from where she stood by the door.

Phoebe sighed. She'd decided on a little defensive spell casting *before* the Halloween party, but she needed both her sisters' help. The fact that she'd actually managed to get both of them up to the attic at the same time seemed encouraging, but so far, agreeing to be in the same room was the extent of her sisters' cooperation. It was clear they were still angry with each other and continuing to fight over the guy Phoebe hadn't even met. What was his name? Oh, yes. Dylan. That was it. All it took was one mention of his name for Prue and Piper to be at each other's throats.

The truth was Phoebe was getting pretty tired of all the bickering. She was facing something far more critical than finding Mr. Right. Not that her sisters' love lives weren't important, of course. But on a scale of one to ten, Phoebe would put her ability to survive October 31 ahead of figuring out who should come first with some guy she'd never even laid eyes on.

"Thank you, Prue. Thank you, Piper," she interrupted before her sisters could use helping her as yet another excuse to argue. "I'm sure you both want to help and I appreciate it very much.

"But what I'd really appreciate," she went on, stepping up behind *The Book of Shadows* and holding out both her hands, "is if we could just take a minute to cast this one little teeny spell."

"Well, of course we can," Piper said, her tone slightly miffed as she came forward to take one of the hands Phoebe held out. "Honestly, Phoebs. There's no reason to treat us as if we're children, you know."

Oh, isn't there? Phoebe thought. Wisely, she held her tongue. Now, if only she could get Prue over here, they could finally get this show on the road.

Prue stepped to the other side of Phoebe and

took her free hand. "What kind of spell are we casting?" she asked.

"It's one to compel spirits to materialize and speak the truth," Phoebe replied. "The one I used before was just a revealing spell, and Charlotte was the only ghost I was able to get to reveal herself.

"What I want to do is to get all *three* ghosts—Betty's, Ronald's, and Charlotte's—to materialize in the same room at the same time. Then the second part of the spell will compel them to tell the truth. And *then* we'll finally know what really happened that night."

"Sounds kind of complicated," Piper commented.

"Makes perfect sense to me," Prue replied.

"Thanks for the support. It was the best I could do on short notice," Phoebe answered swiftly, responding to her sisters' comments in reverse order. Jeez. It was exhausting being a referee all the time. "Now can we please just do the spell?"

"Ready whenever you are," Piper said.

"Go for it," Prue added.

Phoebe hesitated a moment. "Um, you guys—you're going to have to hold hands during this part. It makes the Power of Three connection stronger. You both know that."

Both Prue and Piper's expressions turned sour. For a moment nothing happened. Then Piper stuck out her hand.

"No problem."

Silently, Prue joined hands with Piper, but she didn't look happy about it.

When Phoebe finally met Dylan, she was going to have a thing or two to say to him, she thought. She wanted her sisters back, and she wanted them right now!

She pulled in a deep breath, focusing on the spell.

"Okay," she said. "Here goes."

"You're pinching," Piper complained before Phoebe could go on. Abruptly, she flung Prue's hand away. "I can't do this. She's squeezing too tight."

"Oh, don't be such a wimp," Prue said. "I was not."

Phoebe felt her head begin to pound. She wasn't sure how much more of this sisterly conflict she could take.

"Prue," she began, a little tentatively.

"Oh, fine!" Prue declared dramatically. "Take her side. Well, if the two of you are so close, you don't need me. I can take a hint. I know when I'm not wanted."

She stomped out the attic door.

"Thanks a lot, Piper," Phoebe said.

"Don't blame me because Prue lost her temper," Piper said in a voice loud enough for Prue to hear as she marched down the stairs. "It's not *my* fault."

The sound of Prue's voice drifted back up into the attic.

"Wait a minute! I heard that," Piper cried. "Don't think you can talk to *me* like that, Prue Halliwell!"

She dashed after Prue, her shoes clattering against the stairs. Phoebe was left alone in the attic.

So much for the Power of Three! she decided.

As soon as she sorted out the real story on the Halloween Murders, she was definitely going to have to turn her attention to the mystery of Prue and Piper.

Might as well open my own witch detective agency, Phoebe thought.

She rubbed her empty hands together, staring down at *The Book of Shadows.* She'd just have to do the incantation on her own and hope for the best. Now that she thought about it, that was pretty much what she'd been doing all along.

Phoebe held her hands out, palms down, above *The Book of Shadows.* She recited the incantation in a low, sing-song voice. For a moment, absolutely nothing happened.

Oh, for crying out loud, not again! she thought.

In the next moment, the air at the far end of the attic began to shimmer. That's more like it, Phoebe thought. Soon she'd have her ghosts and she'd have her answers.

The specter seemed to explode straight out of the air.

Uh-oh, Phoebe thought. She was in big trouble now.

The apparition's body was almost formless. Phoebe couldn't tell if it was male or female, which somehow made the wolflike Halloween mask that it wore all the spookier. Of course, the truly spooky thing was the enormous knife in the ghost's right hand.

Slowly, menacingly, the ghost approached Phoebe.

"Keep out," it told her in an inhuman voice that made Phoebe's flesh crawl. "Keep out. Keep away."

"Who are you?" Phoebe asked, her voice shaking.

Then she realized—this was the masked man, the unknown attacker that Charlotte told her about! She was alone in the attic with the perpetrator of the Halloween Murders!

Phoebe shrieked as the ghost took another menacing step toward her, lifted the knife, and brought the blade down toward her chest.

Phoebe dodged right, away from the downward sweep of the knife. It caught the sleeve of her shirt and cut a huge gash in it.

Phoebe's breath caught in her throat. *The ghost may be incorporeal, but that knife is real!* she realized.

She quickly chanted a counterspell she'd taken the precaution of memorizing. The ghost vanished without a trace just as Piper's anxious voice called up the stairs.

"Phoebe? Is anything wrong?"

Phoebe sucked in a shaky breath. Her throat felt parched and sore. "Everything's okay, Piper," she called back.

She wasn't going to try to explain to her sisters what had just happened. They probably weren't capable of stopping their argument long enough for her to tell the story anyhow.

Phoebe closed the attic door with trembling fingers and made her way down to her bedroom. Once there, she lit a meditation candle and settled onto her bed in the lotus position. After a few minutes, she felt herself relax. Her breathing evened out and her heart rate returned to normal.

There was one good thing about what had just happened, Phoebe told herself. In a way, her plan had worked in spite of itself. Now Phoebe knew Charlotte was telling the truth when she'd claimed there was a fourth person in the back room that night, a person whose identity was still unknown.

Now more than ever Phoebe was glad she'd promised to help Charlotte Logan. Charlotte, Ronald, and Betty deserved to be at peace. The truth about what had happened that night in 1958 needed to be told, even though keeping her promise was going to put Phoebe in the gravest danger—perhaps more danger than she'd ever faced on her own before.

Dylan had scored the best table in the Russian Hill café—the one with the postcard-perfect view of the Golden Gate's lights sparkling like a string of golden stars against the night. Not that he cared. He never really understood why mortals got so excited about scenery, anyway. It was all so ephemeral. Did they really think their pretty red bridge would last? Besides, he was here for another sort of view entirely.

He picked up the glass of white wine he had ordered, raised it, and gently swirled the contents. Then he gazed down into the clear whirling liquid.

Specks of color flickered in the wine and then solidified into a miniature but perfect image.

Dylan saw Prue Halliwell in what had to be her bedroom. She was dressed in a nightshirt, curled up in bed, reading a book.

"Oh, no, no," he said softly. "That will never do. Surely we can make better use of your evening, Prue."

Prue shifted restlessly in bed, unable to concentrate on the book she was reading no matter how hard she tried. Thoughts of Dylan and her upcoming date with him at tomorrow night's concert kept running through her mind.

How dare Piper claim she had first right to Dylan, just because he was performing at P3 and just because she'd gotten to him first? As if you could count talking to someone on the telephone.

You couldn't, Prue decided as she shifted in bed once more. After all, who ever heard of "love at first sound"?

Nobody, that's who, Prue thought with satisfaction. But everyone had heard of love at first sight, which only went to prove it was *seeing* someone first that counted.

She intended to make that crystal clear to Piper before all this was over. After all, she was the one who'd seen Dylan first. Even Piper admitted that much. Now it was time Piper admitted defeat and backed off.

Prue closed her eyes and imagined the scene at P3. She would arrive in her best dress—her best *new* dress—looking drop-dead gorgeous. Piper, who would have been working all night, would look tired, disheveled, and sweaty.

Dylan would be in the middle, caught between them. Then, he'd turn and walk toward Prue. He'd take her in his arms . . .

That was the moment Prue's little fantasy was supposed to fade to black. Instead, it kept on going, as if some outside power had added another reel. In the space of about two minutes, Prue's wonderful dream became an absolute nightmare.

That's how long it took for Piper to storm across P3 and snatch Dylan out of Prue's loving arms.

No! Prue thought as she opened her eyes and sat bolt upright. She could feel the heat that always seemed to accompany her thoughts of Dylan coursing through her veins.

There was no way she would ever let Piper take Dylan away.

We're going to settle now, Prue decided. Saturday night was too important. She couldn't afford to take any chances. She threw back the covers and got out of bed. She snatched the can of soda she'd been drinking from her bedside table and took a swig. All that heat pouring through her was making her thirsty.

It wasn't until Prue stormed across the hall and actually barged into Piper's bedroom that she realized her sister wasn't there.

Of course she isn't here, Prue realized. Piper was working. She was still at P3.

Prue told herself she should turn around and march right back out of Piper's room again. After all, she was invading her sister's privacy. But a second wave of heat coursing through her made her linger.

When it came to love, there was no such thing as unfair. All the usual rules were off. She'd do whatever it took to make sure that Dylan was hers, and she wouldn't guilt-out about any of it.

Quietly, Prue moved around Piper's bedroom. Now that she'd decided to conduct a search, she wasn't quite sure what she was looking for. Some sign that Piper was planning the same thing she was, perhaps. That she was going out of her way to look good for tomorrow night, the night when Dylan would make it absolutely clear which Halliwell sister he really wanted.

Maybe she'd see an appointment card for a facial and a manicure. Or, Prue thought, as she spied a familiar shopping bag in front of Piper's closet, maybe her sister had gone shopping!

In a flash, Prue was across the room and had Piper's closet door open. Piper's new dress was hanging in front, face out. Prue felt yet another flash of heat shoot through her at the sight of the slim, white, lacy number. It was the dress from her favorite boutique that she'd planned on buying. But it hadn't been there when Prue went to the boutique on her lunch break. The reason for that was now perfectly clear. Sneaky, underhanded little Piper had beat her to the punch!

Prue reached out to touch the dress, conveniently forgetting that one hand held her can of soda. A cascade of fizzy brown liquid poured across the front of the dress, staining the lacy white fabric.

Prue jerked her hand back. A second spray of soda spattered the contents of Piper's closet. Now not only the new dress, but all of Piper's date clothes were ruined. Prue discovered she was shaking as she backed out of the closet and eased the door closed. As she hurried back to her own room, she could feel her heart pounding.

What did I just do? Prue wondered. She hadn't really meant to ruin the dress, had she? It was just an accident, the kind that could happen to anyone.

Prue plunked her soda can back down on her bedside table and collapsed onto her bed, her head in her hands.

What was happening to her? This kind of behavior just didn't seem normal. She was usually careful, considerate. She wasn't the sort of person who went spilling cola all over her sister's wardrobe.

But the second Prue's eyes were closed, an image of Dylan seemed to fill the inside of her eyelids. Prue's head snapped up. Well, that decided it. What was done was done.

It was too late to worry about Piper's dress now. If spilling a little soda meant Prue was the one who wound up with Dylan, she could live with that.

Prue was smiling as she drifted over to examine her own closet. With Piper's ability to compete seriously impaired, there was nothing to stop Prue from getting what she wanted. By tomorrow night, her fantasy would be complete.

Prue Halliwell would find herself exactly where she wanted to be: in Dylan Thomas's arms.

CHAPTER 8

Piper glanced at her watch as she parked in front of the local dry cleaner. It was five o'clock on Saturday afternoon, which meant she had a little more than an hour to get home, shower, do her hair, makeup, and jewelry, and then get back to P3 for that night's dinner crowd and the Dylan Thomas and the Good Nights concert.

Just thinking about Dylan walking into the club made Piper's heart race. She didn't have Phoebe's gift of seeing the future, but she could tell—tonight was going to be amazing.

She hurried into the dry cleaner and dug out the receipt for her white cashmere shawl. After all, when she and Dylan went out after the concert, she'd need the perfect thing to wear over her new lace dress.

"Here it is, Piper," the woman behind the counter said with a smile. "Oh, I've got some of your sister Prue's things ready, too. Do you want to take them for her?"

Piper hesitated for a moment. Considering the way Prue had been acting lately, doing a favor for her was not high on Piper's priority list. Still, they usually helped each other out this way, and it seemed petty to say no.

"Sure," Piper said. "I'll take her stuff."

"That will be seven dollars for the shawl and thirty-four for your sister's things."

"Thirty-four dollars?"

"Well, she's got two sweaters, two suits, and a dress."

"That figures." Piper sighed and dug into her wallet. She could hardly refuse now, but Prue would owe her for this one.

"Thanks," she said, taking the dry cleaning.

"Are you working tonight?" the woman called as Piper headed for the door.

"Definitely," Piper replied with a smile. And then she added silently, I intend to play.

In his hotel suite Dylan Thomas carefully placed his guitar in its leather case. He checked his reflection in the mirror. Black jeans, one of his fitted silk shirts, and a long black leather duster that would come off about ten minutes after he took the stage. He liked playing the musician, and he loved the way both Prue and Piper Halliwell seemed so turned on by it. Piper gazed at him completely star-struck even in the middle of the routine sound check.

Dylan glanced at his watch. "Maybe it's time I checked in on dear little Piper," he murmured to himself. "After all, I've got to make sure she's getting ready for our big night."

Before he called up the vision that would allow him to watch her, though, he decided on some extra insurance.

He walked over to the black candle that he'd placed in the silver candlestick. He drew a slash in the air above it, and the candle lit itself. Next he took a pinch of silvery dust from the small leather pouch that lay next to the candlestick. Quietly, he began a Latin incantation while he sprinkled the silvery dust around the top of the candle.

Dylan smiled with satisfaction as the silvery dust remained suspended, forming a perfect ring around the flame, then began to glow a bright, hot white.

"So will the power of my spell intensify," Dylan murmured. "As the flame is circled by magic, so shall Piper Halliwell be encircled by white-hot rage. Until she—like the candle—is consumed."

"Oh, my God! It's ruined!"

Piper stood in front of her closet, surveying the damage to the dress she'd spent a small fortune on the day before, the one she'd chosen so carefully to make an impression on Dylan.

The whole front of what had been a pristine white lace dress the last time Piper checked was now covered in dark brown splotches. Not only that, whatever had stained the front of the dress also seemed to be on virtually everything else in Piper's closet. Piper literally didn't have a thing to wear.

She slammed the closet door shut and paced around her room. Now, who did she have to thank for this particular turn of events? she wondered. Not that she really needed anyone else to supply the answer to her question. She was perfectly capable of figuring it out all by herself.

It didn't exactly take a rocket scientist.

How could this happen now? It was Saturday night, *the* Saturday night. All that afternoon Piper had worked like a dog to get P3 ready for the official opening of Dylan and the Good Nights. Since she'd worn grubbies to do that, it hadn't occurred to her to check her closet.

Piper's original plan, most of which she'd actually been able to accomplish, had been to leave early, pick up her shawl, then come home and take a nice bubble bath filled with her most enticing scent before putting on that perfect dress and her highest heels. Okay, she'd gotten stuck in traffic, which meant trading in the bath for a shower. Still, she'd arrived home, looking forward to putting on her killer outfit, then heading back to P3 and knocking Prue out of the ballpark at the same time she knocked Dylan's socks off!

Instead, Piper was the one who'd been knocked out, and she hadn't even seen the punch coming!

We'll just see about that, she decided. She felt a quick pulse of white-hot heat surge through her blood. If Prue thought ruining Piper's dress would make her give up, she was sadly mistaken. Piper had a secret weapon, one she wasn't afraid to use.

Quickly, she ran downstairs and retrieved the dry cleaning she'd just picked up. She'd taken her shawl up to her room but left Prue's things hanging from the banister.

Piper lifted the plastic garment bag that covered Prue's things and flipped through the hangers. Two boring business suits—no good. A red cable-knit turtleneck—not helpful. A long taupe cardigan—ditto. And the dress?

Piper started laughing when she saw the dress. Her luck couldn't be better! Because she'd picked up Prue's favorite party dress. It was basic black and strapless, a total knockout.

As soon as she spotted it, Piper knew what her sister had in mind. Prue was going to wear her classic "little black dress" to make her own impression on Dylan.

"Sorry, sister dear," Piper murmured. "But I really think it would look much better on me."

Piper was humming as she took the dress up to her room. She could just imagine the look on Prue's face when she went to pick up her favorite dress, only to be told that it wasn't there anymore because Piper had picked it up for her!

This was working out even better than she'd planned, Piper thought as she wriggled into the slithery black sheath. She felt no guilt. Didn't they say that possession was nine-tenths of the law? If so, this was *her* dress now. The only way Prue was going to get it off her was to rip it off. Piper could hardly wait to see the look on Dylan's face when he saw her in it—and the look on Prue's when she realized what Piper had done.

This will teach her to mess with my things, Piper thought. She swept up her hair into a classic, elegant twist and pinned it with a comb, then added long, sparkling rhinestone earrings. She smiled as she went into the bathroom to put the finishing touches on her makeup.

Even another traffic jam on the way back to P3 couldn't ruin Piper's mood of sweet anticipation. By the time she got back to the club, it was packed. She could hardly get in the door. The dance floor was filled with bodies, all doing elaborate steps, turns, and lifts in time to the music. Piper had to admit swing dancing looked like a lot of fun. Best of all, it was real partner dancing, the kind where the guy took the girl in his arms.

I'll bet Dylan is as good at the dancing part as he is at the singing, Piper thought as she elbowed her way through the crowd. She could hardly wait to find out for herself.

She spotted Prue standing at the edge of the dance floor where she had an unimpeded view of the band. She was wearing a slinky little red dress, and she had a bouquet of long-stemmed white roses in her arms.

At the sight of her, Piper could feel her blood begin to boil. There was only one person who could have given Prue those flowers, unless she'd brought them with her, of course. Personally, Piper wouldn't put it past her.

"Don't you think that dress is just a little tacky?" Piper asked as she stepped to Prue's side. The band was playing a slow number so she didn't have to shout. Not that she would have minded.

"Red is so . . . obvious," Piper went on. "But I don't know—maybe you *want* your dress to shout, 'Look at me, look at me, look at me!' "

Prue glanced down at her, malice bright in her blue eyes. If she was upset to see Piper wearing her very best dress, she did a good job of hiding it.

"They wear black to funerals," she said sweetly. "Guess this is yours."

"Ha!" Piper said, wishing desperately she could think of a snappier comeback. "Dream on."

Prue lifted the rose blossoms to her nose and gave a delicate sniff. "These are from Dylan," she said. "Aren't they lovely?" She held them out toward Piper. "Go ahead. Smell."

Piper felt a hot flush spread throughout her body. It was all she could do not to tear the flowers away from Prue and trample them on the dance floor.

"I hear a guy always gives really expensive

flowers when he's done something wrong," Piper finally said. "Maybe those are your consolation prize."

"Fat chance," Prue said, her eyes flashing.

Oh, it was just too perfect, Dylan thought.

He could see Prue and Piper facing off from his position on the raised band platform. Prue definitely looked as if she had fire in her eyes. Piper looked as if she'd love to tear the roses right out of Prue's arms.

Good thing he'd taken the precaution of asking the florist to remove the thorns, Dylan thought. He'd hate for Prue to be hurt if Piper lost control and gave into her impulse. Dylan didn't want Piper to hurt Prue.

If anyone is going to hurt the Charmed Ones, it's going to be me, Dylan thought.

He signaled to the band, and they launched into a rollicking dance number. The crowd at P3 roared with delight as even more bodies began to gyrate on the dance floor. But even through the enthusiastic crowd, Dylan could still see the Halliwell sisters, arguing about him. They were toe-to-toe now.

He took a deep breath and used his powers to tune out the sounds around him until all he could hear was Prue and Piper.

"It's a fight to the finish then," he heard Piper declare.

"A fight to the finish," Prue echoed. She thrust

out her hand. Piper took it, and the two sisters shook on their pact. Then Piper turned and walked away.

Excellent, Dylan thought as he let his hearing return to normal. This was all turning out even better than he'd planned.

Prue and Piper were practically at each other's throats. It shouldn't take very much to send them over the edge into action. To get them to translate their murderous thoughts into murderous deeds. If he could do that, they'd take care of each other themselves. Dylan wouldn't even have to kill them. They'd kill each other for him!

Perhaps it was because the sisters already had such strong feelings about one another, he mused as the band finished the dance number. Piper and Prue were already tuned to each other's energy. It was probably part of what made them the Charmed Ones. But now their own closeness was working against them. And for him. They had been pathetically easy to divide and conquer.

"Time for a love song," he announced, cueing the band into a slower number. The sax player began the quiet opening riff, but Dylan barely noticed. He was completely focused on the Halliwell sisters. His spells were working so well, there really wasn't much more he had to do. Still, he couldn't resist stoking the fire.

"I'd like to dedicate this song to the woman who's made our appearance here possible tonight," he purred into the microphone. "Let me hear a big hand of thanks for the owner of P3, Miss Piper Halliwell!"

Dylan watched in satisfaction as Piper beamed and Prue scowled.

Soon, very soon now, it would be time to finish what he'd started.

"You can't have him! He's mine!"

The strident voice cut through the low murmur of students decorating Thayer Hall. From her position near the old fireplace mantel where she'd been hanging black crepe paper, Phoebe started. Who could that be? she wondered.

"Don't think you can ignore me, Phoebe Halliwell," the voice went on, this time a little closer. "Brett's mine, and I'm not going to let you have him."

Here we go again! Phoebe thought as she belatedly recognized the angry voice as belonging to Brett's ex-girlfriend. Phoebe hadn't been alone with Brett since their little misunderstanding in the study hall, which was just fine with her, thank you very much.

Sighing, she turned to face Wendy Chang and saw that Wendy's face was flushed with anger, and her eyes were hot and bright. I wonder if anything I say will get through to her, Phoebe wondered. Still, she had to try.

"Look, Wendy," she said, deciding to be blunt. "You don't have anything to worry about. I don't want Brett—at all."

Wendy's eyes narrowed. "I saw you this afternoon at the costume shop," she said accusingly. "You rented that lavender dress. You know that's what you chose because you think Brett won't be able to resist you in it!"

"What?" Phoebe asked, stunned. She'd rented the long lavender dress because it was the only costume that looked vaguely fifties-ish. Its tight bodice and full skirt reminded her a little of the pink one that Charlotte had worn. She'd thought that maybe with a rhinestone tiara, she could come to the party as a princess.

"Well, it won't work," Wendy went on, her voice low and furious. "Because no matter what you wear, you can't have him. You can't go to the Halloween party with Brett. He's mine."

I heard you the first time, Phoebe thought. Was this girl certifiable?

"You're making a mistake, Wendy," Phoebe tried again. "I'm not trying to attract Brett, and I'm *not* going to the party with him. Even if he asked me to, I wouldn't."

"Of course, you're denying it." Wendy took a couple of steps closer, her fists clenching and unclenching at her sides. "You're such a liar."

Phoebe felt a shiver of fear scoot down her spine. Her back was to the wall. She had nowhere to go, and she didn't really know the other students on the decorating committee all that well. Would anyone believe her if she said something like, "Excuse me, but we've got a psycho here"?

Without warning, Wendy erupted into action. She darted toward Phoebe, reached behind her, and ripped down the crepe paper chain that Phoebe had just pinned up.

"This is what I'll do to you if you try to take him away from me!" Wendy shouted, tearing the crepe paper into tiny pieces and hurling it to the floor.

"All right, that's enough," Stan Morrison said. Stan, a tall, easygoing senior, was one of the party's organizers. He put a restraining hand on Wendy's arm. "I think you need to chill," he said in a gentle voice.

"Don't tell me what to do," Wendy Chang snarled. She tried to shake off Stan's hand.

"Okay, now," Stan said. "Take it easy. Just calm down." He began to escort Wendy from the room, a quick motion of his head summoning a couple of other students to his side.

"You remember what I told you!" Wendy shouted as she was led away. "Stay away from him or you'll be sorry!"

"Wow!" a girl standing near Phoebe said when Wendy was out of sight. "Do you think she was on something?"

Only her own jealousy, Phoebe thought. Were Prue and Piper going to end up like that? she wondered.

"I don't know," Phoebe told the girl. "I just hope that what I was saying gets through to her, eventually."

"I wouldn't count on that, if I were you," said a new voice.

Phoebe jumped, then turned, embarrassed. How come everybody was sneaking up on her all of a sudden?

"I'm sorry, Phoebe," Marjorie Yarnell said when she saw Phoebe's expression. "I didn't mean to startle you."

"Yeah, well, join the crowd," Phoebe murmured.

Marjorie glanced around the room. "All this black crepe paper," she said. "It seems so . . . grim."

"It's the same decorating scheme they used back in 1958," Stan said cheerfully as he walked back into the room. "We're re-creating a classic."

As he went to the tape deck and popped in an Elvis tape, Marjorie took Phoebe by one arm and led her to a far corner of the room.

"I still think this party is a bad idea, Phoebe. I still think you should try to stop it," Marjorie continued.

"What makes you think I can?" Phoebe asked. She gestured toward the rest of the decorating committee. "This party wasn't my idea. Maybe you should talk to *them.*"

Marjorie's lower lip trembled. "They'll think I'm just a crazy old lady," she said. "I thought . . . I thought that since you've been researching the murders, you'd understand that holding this party is just asking for trouble."

Phoebe studied the older woman curiously. She still hadn't figured out why touching Marjorie's shoulder had triggered that first vision. "Why are you so convinced of that?" she asked.

"That girl in our class, the one who was just in here—what's her name?" Marjorie asked.

"Wendy," Phoebe answered.

"Wendy. She's jealous of you, isn't she?"

Phoebe nodded, not quite sure where this was going. Marjorie wasn't losing it, too, was she?

"Did you ever stop to think—" Marjorie began, then broke off as if she were trying to figure out just how to make her point. "The more I think about the murders," Marjorie continued, "the more I wonder whether they weren't about jealousy. What if someone was determined to break up Betty and Ronald?"

Phoebe thought of the masked ghost in the attic and also of her interview with Dean Williams. Then again, the ghost in the attic couldn't have been Dean Williams. Dean Williams was alive.

"You mean some guy who was angry because Betty loved Ronald instead of him?" Phoebe asked.

Marjorie was silent for a moment. "I don't know," she said at last. "It could have been someone like that. Or someone like that Wendy Chang."

"You mean, Ronald had a jealous ex?"

Phoebe's mind whirled with the possibilities. She hadn't found anything to indicate that, but maybe she just hadn't been asking the right questions.

Personally, though, Phoebe would put her money on the unknown assailant—the guy in the mask—as the prime candidate for the suspect who lost it due to jealousy.

She could hardly mention that to Marjorie, though. So far, only Phoebe and Charlotte knew about the guy in the mask. Phoebe wanted to keep his presence a secret until after the party.

Then, if the events of 1958 really did replay themselves the way she and Charlotte hoped, she'd be able to tell Marjorie, and the whole world, about him and clear Ronald Galvez.

"I think that's an interesting theory," Phoebe told Marjorie. "But I don't think it's reason enough to call off the party. Nobody is mocking what happened in 1958, you know. We're not trying to be disrespectful. Nothing bad will happen. You'll see. In fact, the outcome of the party just might surprise you."

"I hope you're right," Marjorie said, sounding more nervous than ever. "But I can see that nothing I say will change your mind, so I'll let you get on with your work and stop bothering you. Good luck, Phoebe."

Without another word, she turned and walked away.

"Thanks," Phoebe said to Marjorie's retreating

back, slightly mystified by the older woman's parting words. Not that she didn't appreciate them, of course. Personally, Phoebe had a feeling she was going to need all the luck that she could get.

She watched as Marjorie walked through the doorway, narrowly missing a collision with one of Phoebe's co-workers on the decorating committee. Phoebe recognized her as the girl who'd commented on Wendy Chang's behavior.

The girl came into the room, then stopped dead. Her face turned sheet white.

"For heaven's sake," Phoebe said as she moved toward her swiftly. "What's wrong? What happened?"

Had Wendy Chang actually hurt someone?

Phoebe skidded to a stop as the girl raised one arm and pointed over Phoebe's right shoulder. She could hardly hold her arm up, her body was shaking so badly. Phoebe swung around and felt her own knees begin to shake.

Something was written on the wall behind her right above where she'd stood just moments before, discussing the events of that horrible night in 1958 with Marjorie. It was something Phoebe was absolutely certain hadn't been there before.

Just one word.

Beware!

Written in dripping red letters.

CHAPTER 9

Dylan flashed a smile at a girl dancing close to the stage, but he kept an eye on the Halliwell sisters. They'd progressed from scowls to sniping remarks to what Dylan classified as a pre-hair-pulling fight.

At the moment Prue was in sabotage mode. Dylan had watched with enjoyment as throughout the evening Prue had done her best to create small but annoying "accidents." All of them required Piper's immediate attention and kept her focus away from Dylan.

A few minutes ago, Prue had "accidentally" stepped backward into a waiter who was carrying a tray filled with drinks. The glasses crashed to the floor, soaking the floor and half a dozen customers. Piper was there in an instant, apologizing to the customers and directing the cleanup.

Now Dylan watched as a new gleam entered Prue's ice blue eyes as she spotted a woman with razor-cut short blond hair. She was wearing a white wool suit and sitting at a table with two other women.

I wonder who she is, Dylan thought. Prue obviously knows. She was heading straight toward her.

Again, Dylan altered his hearing, so that the music of his band faded into the distance and what he heard was the conversation at the table.

"What do you think, Raina?" asked one of the other women at the table. "Are you going to give P3 a good review in tomorrow's paper?"

The woman with the razor cut shrugged. "So far, so good," she said. "Can't complain about the food or the music, but we haven't had dessert yet so the jury's still out."

Oh, I predict a memorable dessert, Dylan thought. A waiter bringing a tray filled with cakes and pies was headed straight toward them. And Prue was right behind him.

It was so perfect, he almost couldn't bear to watch.

But he did, of course.

The waiter held out the dessert tray and began introducing that evening's offerings. He was totally unaware of Prue, bending down beside him to adjust the strap on her shoe. A second later, she straightened up, managing to catch her shoulder beneath the edge of the tray.

The waiter stared in horror as the tray tilted and the beautiful, frosted desserts slid directly into the reviewer's lap.

"You clod!" Raina screamed. "You idiot!"

Dylan felt a grudging admiration for Prue as she slipped discretely into the crowd. That was so slick, so well timed, nearly worthy of a warlock. He signaled to the band to lower the volume, so that the critic's voice could carry clearly throughout the club.

"You just wait to see what kind of review this club gets in tomorrow's paper!" she ranted. "No one in the entire Bay Area will ever want to walk in here."

The expression of horror on Piper's face was worth it all.

"No!" she cried, rushing over to the critic's table. "Please, let me apologize. And say that I'd be happy to pay for dry-cleaning your suit or—"

Not bad, Dylan thought. But it could be even more fun. Let's see if we can make the action a little more interesting. . . .

"Prue Halliwell," Piper's voice called. "I demand that you let me out of here right this instant!"

In your dreams, Prue thought. "I don't know what you're talking about," she called through the locked door of P3's employee bathroom. "The door just locked on its own behind me when I closed it. Let me see if I can find someone who has a key."

There! That ought to hold Piper for a while. A long while, if Prue had her way. With a smile on her carefully made-up face, Prue hurried back out to the dance floor, the need to find a P3 staff member with a key to the bathroom conveniently slipping her mind.

She'd remember eventually, she told herself. Like, say, for instance, right after Dylan had asked her out for the rest of the evening. In the meantime, Prue intended to take advantage of every second her sister was out of the way.

Prue's nerves were humming with excitement by the time she reached the dance floor and once more found the perfect spot from which to watch Dylan as he sang. He had such a wonderful voice. Prue could have sworn he'd sung every love song just for her.

All in all, the evening wasn't going badly. She'd divided her time pretty evenly between watching Dylan and doing her best to keep Piper out of the way.

By the time she managed to lock Piper in the bathroom, Piper had been looking harried and exhausted. Prue, on the other hand, knew she looked as good as she had when the evening started.

She patted her beaded evening bag. That's where the key to the restroom was safely hidden and would stay—until she felt like letting Piper out.

Dylan ended the song he was singing and bowed to the burst of applause that followed.

"Thank you. Thank you, ladies and gentlemen," he said. The applause quieted, then swelled again as, one by one, Dylan introduced his fellow band members.

"I know I mentioned this when we started," he went on when the applause for the band was over, "but I'd like to give a second round of thanks to the person who's opened her club to us all week, the owner of P3, Miss Piper Halliwell. Piper—come on up here and take a bow!"

Prue felt a quick stab of guilt when she realized Piper was going to miss a well-deserved moment in the spotlight. Just as quickly, she squashed it. Surely there'd be lots of other bands who would thank Piper in public, but there was only one Mr. Right. Only one Dylan Thomas.

"Where is she? Where's Piper?" Prue heard Dylan ask as he directed the spotlight that had been on him to sweep the audience. "Wait a minute—here she comes," he said.

No! Prue thought. It wasn't possible!

Piper stepped up onto the platform beside Dylan and took a bow. Prue felt as if she was choking.

How had Piper gotten out of the bathroom so quickly? One of her staff members must have found her. Now all Prue's plans were in danger of being ruined, unless she acted equally quickly.

She made her way to the band platform just as Dylan and Piper were stepping down from it.

"Congratulations!" she told Piper brightly.

Piper smiled and linked her arm through Dylan's. "Hi, Prue," she said. "Are you all right? You look a little funny."

Ha ha, Prue thought. She gave a trill of bright, false laughter. "Of course I'm all right," she said. "But *you,*" Prue went on, switching her attention to Dylan. "All those sets. You must be exhausted."

"Actually, it's just the opposite," Dylan said as he reached out to tuck Prue's hand through his other arm. Behind Dylan's back, Prue flashed Piper a quick look of triumph. "I always find performing to be energizing, exciting. Particularly when it goes as well as it did tonight."

"All the more reason to find someplace special to go afterward," Prue put in quickly, leaning close to him. "Someplace quiet and romantic. A change from this scene."

"You know, Prue," Dylan said. "That's a great idea."

Prue felt her pulse begin to race. She was pretty sure she knew what was coming. Dylan would ask her out, and together they'd create just the kind of finish to the evening she'd been describing. She could hardly wait to see the look on Piper's face when he did.

She heard Dylan's voice, low and seductive. "So what would you say to finding a place like that right now—Piper?"

Prue jerked back, her body turning hot and

cold by turns, as if Dylan had just dumped a bucket of water over her.

He couldn't have asked Piper out for a romantic evening, could he? Not when he'd just finished telling her what a great idea it was. Not only that, it was *her* great idea.

"I'd love to, Dylan," Piper said. "You'll excuse us, won't you, Prue?"

"But you can't just leave P3!" Prue blurted out. She knew she sounded desperate, but she didn't care. "It's your club. Your responsibility. Don't you have to close up or something?"

Piper shook her head. "My assistant manager can do that for me."

"But—" Prue protested. Then made herself stop as she felt Dylan's beautiful blue eyes upon her.

What was she doing? she wondered.

It was one thing to argue with Piper over Dylan in the privacy of their own home. Arguing over him in public with Dylan actually present—well, that was an entirely different story. Continuing to protest now would only make Prue look childish and stupid.

"I hope you have a lovely time," she said, although the words almost choked her. To her surprise, she felt Dylan's fingers brush against hers.

"I'll see you tomorrow, won't I?" he leaned down to whisper in her ear.

"That depends on what happens tonight, doesn't it?" Prue whispered back.

It wasn't quite as good as being the one he'd chosen tonight, but it was something. If Dylan called Prue tomorrow, she'd know that his date with Piper had been a dud, which just might be the optimal outcome. Piper gets her date, and then Dylan still chooses me. Then Piper would have to admit that she'd lost this little competition.

As Prue released her hold on Dylan's arm and stepped away, she realized she was smiling. Given Piper's track record where guys were concerned, chances were good Prue would hear from Dylan the next day.

Meantime, she had better things to do than mope over the fact that he'd chosen Piper tonight instead of her.

Things like figuring out the very best way to rub Piper's nose in her defeat when Dylan called *her,* Prue, tomorrow.

"So you don't mind me walking you across half the city?" Dylan asked Piper.

"No, honestly," Piper said. They were strolling arm-in-arm, window-shopping, the way couples in love always did in romantic movies. "Usually on a Saturday night I'm at the club till three in the morning. This is such a great break."

"Walking is the way I come back down to earth after a performance," Dylan confessed. "Besides, it's a gorgeous night."

It was one of those rare San Francisco nights without even a trace of fog, just stars glittering high above the city. Piper gazed up, laughing softly to herself. Dylan might be returning to earth, but as far as Piper was concerned every step she took was one closer to the stars. She couldn't remember the last time she'd felt so happy.

"So," Dylan said, his voice sounding hesitant. "Do you think I could persuade you to walk a little farther?"

Piper pulled her cashmere shawl more tightly around her shoulders. "What did you have in mind?"

He ran a gentle hand across her cheekbone. "Why don't we go back to my hotel?"

Piper's heart beat faster at the suggestion.

Dylan had had a choice between the two oldest Halliwell sisters, and he hadn't chosen Prue. He'd chosen her. Now he'd done the one thing Piper was certain would upset Prue most of all. When she found out Dylan had invited Piper back to his hotel, Prue was going to be absolutely furious.

Piper smiled up at Dylan. "I'd love to see your hotel," she said. "Is it far?"

Dylan shook his head. "We can be there in next to no time."

About twenty minutes later, Piper was standing in the living room of Dylan's opulent hotel suite, staring out at the lights of San Francisco. With every second Piper felt more and more as though she really was in a romantic movie. Everything seemed absolutely perfect.

Then Dylan was standing next to her. "I'm so

glad you're here," he said. His lips pressed softly against the side of her neck. Piper jumped a little at the chill it sent racing through her. Then somehow one of her long rhinestone earrings snagged a strand of her hair.

"Ow," she said, disentangling her earring and as she did so, pulling a thick strand of hair out of the comb that held it in place. Great. The entire right side of her carefully upswept hairdo was now falling down around her ears.

"Um, I'd better fix my hair," she said.

"Don't." Dylan's fingers circled her wrist. "It looks great down, kind of wild."

Piper knew she looked a mess, which was a serious obstacle to feeling like a romantic movie heroine. "It'll just take me a minute," she promised, and pulled out of Dylan's grasp.

She closed the bathroom door behind her and turned on the light. "Movie star, ha. I look like a clown," Piper murmured as she took a brush from her bag and began to redo her hair.

She leaned forward and peered more closely into the mirror. Her face looked different to her. Her mouth had a hard, almost mean set to it, and there was something bleak and cold in her eyes that she'd never noticed before.

Feeling a sudden need to look a little more normal, she took off her rhinestone bracelet and slipped it into her bag. What's happened to me? she wondered. And what am I doing here?

It wasn't that she didn't want to be with Dylan

anymore. She did. Or at least, she thought she did. But now that she was away from Dylan's sheer physical presence, Piper felt as if she were waking up from some long, strange dream. Without Dylan by her side to remind her, she couldn't quite seem to recall just what it was that had seemed so important about him.

It's just nerves, that's all, she told herself. Dylan *was* important to her. He had to be. Hadn't she alienated her older sister over him?

She'd ignored her younger sister, too, Piper realized suddenly. She rubbed her forehead, as if to encourage her brain to start working in its old familiar paths again.

There had been something Phoebe wanted to tell her, something she wanted her to do. But Piper couldn't even remember what that something had been.

She heard a gentle knocking on the bathroom door. "Piper? You okay in there?"

"Fine," she called. "I'll be right out."

She washed her face quickly, glad to rinse off the makeup. She felt an urgent need to be herself again—whoever that was.

Taking a deep breath, she stepped back into the living room where she heard a soft pop. She spun around, startled. Dylan stood across the room from her, a newly opened bottle of champagne in his hand.

"I thought we'd have something special to celebrate this incredible night," he said.

Piper watched as he poured the golden, frothy champagne into the two elegant fluted glasses.

The champagne must have already been in the hotel room, and she just hadn't noticed, Piper realized as she watched him settle the bottle back into its silver ice bucket. She knew she hadn't heard anyone from room service come in.

That meant Dylan had planned out the whole evening ahead of time, right down to the romantic candles burning throughout the suite and the crystal vase of long-stemmed red roses on a marble-topped table.

Piper remembered how smug Prue had been over the white roses Dylan had given her at P3. How jealous she, herself, had been. Without warning, a horrible question popped to the forefront of Piper's brain.

Did it even matter to Dylan which Halliwell sister he was with? Prue was wearing red, Piper black. White roses were a pretty safe bet no matter what they had been wearing. Had Dylan decided to which sister to give the roses on the spur of the moment?

Piper watched Dylan's reflection in the windows as he came toward her, balancing two champagne glasses effortlessly in one hand. With the other, he reached to pluck a rose from the vase. When he reached her, he ran the bloodred blossom slowly along Piper's bare back.

She shivered at the touch of the downy petals.

Gently but firmly, Dylan turned her to face

him. He handed her one of the champagne glasses. "To the success of this evening," he said, raising his glass in a toast.

Piper clinked her glass against his. The first sip of champagne made her head swim. All of a sudden, the room felt way too close—and Dylan even closer. He took a step toward her and bent his head.

He's going to kiss me, Piper thought. At the very last second, she stepped back.

"Ummm . . . wait!" she exclaimed, trying not to notice how incredibly lame she sounded.

"Wait?"

She nodded, racking her brain for an excuse. "I—I didn't eat anything before going to work tonight," she said hurriedly. "That little bit of champagne just went right to my head and I—I just remembered I left my bracelet in the bathroom." That didn't even make sense, she realized, but she kept talking. "I'd better go get it. I'll be right back."

Dylan's expression was unreadable as he looked down at her. He probably thought she was nuts.

Piper set down her champagne glass and made her way back to the bathroom. Once there, she closed her eyes and leaned her forehead against the cool glass of the mirror.

Piper opened her eyes and faced her reflection. She still saw that hardness in her mouth, though her eyes looked more like her own again. What was going on with her? Quickly, she took the rhinestone bracelet from her purse and slipped it on.

Silently, Piper eased the bathroom door open and peered out, but she couldn't see Dylan anywhere.

Maybe he went to refill his champagne glass, Piper thought. She could see hers plainly, right where she'd left it on the table.

In the next moment, Piper backed up a step, clapping her hand over her mouth to muffle her startled exclamation.

Now Dylan was standing by the table, too. But he hadn't walked over. He'd *blinked* himself there. In Piper's experience, that could mean only one thing.

Dylan Thomas was a warlock!

No wonder I didn't want to kiss him, Piper thought. Her instincts might have been a little slow but, fortunately, they had shown up in the nick of time.

As Piper watched, Dylan took a black velvet pouch from an inner pocket of his jacket. He opened it and poured a bit of bright red powder into his hand. With his other hand he held her champagne glass in front of the candle's flame. "By darkness and light, by flame burning bright, the Charmed One's heart shall be mine, from this eve and through time," Dylan murmured as he poured the powder into the glass.

Heart thundering, Piper watched the air above her glass sparkle, first white, then red, then black.

So that's how he's doing it, she realized. He'd given her some sort of potion, and she'd be willing to bet her last cent he'd done the same to Prue. No wonder they were fighting over him! He'd been controlling them, playing them against each other all along. The old divide-and-conquer routine.

Piper shuddered when she thought of how close Dylan's scheme had come to working.

"To the success of the evening," she heard him murmur as he returned the pouch to the pocket of his jacket. Piper felt her blood boil—this time with anger.

We'll just see about that, she vowed. Silently, she slipped out of the bathroom and back into the living room.

Then she lifted her hands in a time freeze.

She smiled as the handsome warlock froze in place, the champagne flute halfway to his mouth.

Quickly, Piper grabbed her shawl and made her escape, resisting the temptation to dump the vase of long-stemmed red roses over Dylan's head on the way out.

He'd figure out she was gone soon enough. In the meantime, Piper had more important things to do—like getting home to her sisters and telling Prue the truth.

Phoebe flopped over onto her stomach on the sofa, trying to get comfortable while she watched late-night TV. Weren't Prue and Piper ever coming home? she wondered. Even though they hadn't been much help lately, she was willing to overlook that. Tonight she really needed to talk to them.

The events of her decorating session had unnerved her, Phoebe had to admit. Even when Stan Morrison had come back in and sponged away the word *Beware*, Phoebe couldn't help seeing it in her mind's eye every time she looked at the wall. She had no idea how it had gotten there. Had Wendy written it—or had the message come from the masked ghost?

Either way, she'd been extremely grateful when Stan had said she could go home. In spite of her reassurances to Marjorie Yarnell, Phoebe was definitely starting to get the creeps about what might happen tomorrow night. She knew there was only one thing that could make her feel better: her sisters' support.

Too bad they weren't around to offer some.

Phoebe felt a tendril of icy air creep down her back. Honestly, she thought in irritation. The heat wasn't on the fritz again, was it? Halliwell Manor was an old house. Basics like heating and plumbing could be temperamental at times and always at the most inopportune moments.

When Phoebe felt a second blast of icy air, she decided she'd better check the thermostat. Grumpily, she got up.

The masked ghost from the attic stood directly behind the couch. Waiting for her.

Phoebe froze in place, her heart pounding. Apparently, the incantation she'd used before had only discouraged the spirit, not sent it away permanently.

"I warned you again today," the figure whispered in a voice that sent chills running over every inch of Phoebe's body. "I warned you! But you didn't listen. Now you'll have to pay the price."

The ghost lunged toward her.

Phoebe faltered, almost tripping backward over the coffee table in the process. Now was hardly the time to forget the way the living room furniture was arranged, she mentally chastised herself. She ought to be able to outsmart this specter. After all, they were in her house.

The only trouble was, ghosts could do things Phoebe couldn't. Like walk straight *through* the furniture. The knife the ghost carried whistled through the air as he swung it down.

The ghost's body might be insubstantial, Phoebe thought as she dodged out into the hallway, but that knife sure seemed real enough. Phoebe didn't want it near any part of her.

"Who are you?" she shouted. "What do you want?"

"Beware!" the ghost intoned. "Beware!"

Then it rushed straight for her.

CHAPTER 10

Phoebe turned and ran for the front door. Just as she reached it, to her astonishment and dismay, it opened. Piper stepped across the threshold.

"Phoebe, Prue, I'm— Yikes!" Piper called out.

Instinctively, she threw her hands up. The ghost froze in midair, the knife he clenched in one upraised fist gleaming in the bright light of the hall.

Piper stepped around him cautiously then shot Phoebe an inquiring look. "Bad date?"

"Ha ha," Phoebe answered. "Very funny."

"Seriously, Phoebs," Piper said as she closed the door and stepped a little closer. She shuddered as she got a good look at the knife. "What's going on? Who is this guy?"

"I don't even know if it is a guy," Phoebe

answered. "But it definitely fits the murderous ghost category. And what's going on is what I've been trying to tell you about for days now. It's the reason I need your help—and Prue's."

"Okay, okay," Piper said. "I'm sorry." Her expression hardened as she stared at the spirit. "So what's the deal here, Phoebs? How come you've got a ghost attacking you?"

"I think it doesn't want me to expose it as the real perpetrator of the Halloween Murders," Phoebe said. She eyed the ghost a little doubtfully. "How long will this freeze last?"

"I'm not sure," Piper admitted. "So talk fast."

Quickly, Phoebe filled Piper in on her investigation.

"Wow!" Piper said. "I can see why you'd want a little backup for this. Sounds like pretty major stuff. So, shall we zap the grisly ghost into a million pieces, give or take a few?"

"Tempting, but we can't do that," Phoebe said. "At least not yet. Whoever this spirit is, I need it around tomorrow night so I can witness what really happened."

"Well, if you're sure," Piper said doubtfully.

"Banishing it from the house would be okay, though," Phoebe went on. "I'm getting kind of tired of being on the receiving end of sneak attacks."

"Banishment it is," Piper said.

Without warning, the ghost came unfrozen and hurtled toward Phoebe.

"Not so fast, pal!" Piper exclaimed. She froze it

again. "Quick, Phoebe," she instructed. "Take my hand."

Phoebe grasped Piper's right hand, tightly. It was good to have at least one of her sisters on her side again. Now, if only they could get Prue as well, things would be back to normal and Phoebe could relax.

Okay, well maybe not *relax*, exactly. But she'd feel a whole lot better.

In a low voice, Piper chanted an incantation. After the first time, Phoebe chimed in, chanting along, adding her power to Piper's. "Back to realms of darkness vanish. You from these four walls, I banish. Nevermore here appear to me. As I will, so must it be."

The ghost came unfrozen once more. But before it could get to Phoebe and Piper, the incantation took effect. With a howl of rage and despair, it vanished.

"Hey, not bad for the Power of Two," Piper commented.

"Wait a minute," Phoebe said, walking forward slowly and carefully to where the ghost had been just moments before. "It left something behind."

She knelt to retrieve the knife that had fallen to the floor of the hallway. Phoebe had been sure that it was real, and she was right. Now she held it in her hand.

The vision hit her like a ton of bricks.

Phoebe froze in place as the familiar surrounding of Halliwell Manor faded all around her. *Where am I?* she wondered. Then, with a start, she realized exactly where she was.

She was in Thayer Hall in 1958—at the Halloween party.

The vision was incredibly detailed, one of the most powerful Phoebe had ever experienced. No longer was she merely an onlooker. Now it was almost as if she was a part of the scene. The walls were draped in black crepe paper. Jack-o'-lanterns flickered, casting eerie shadows across the room. A long table held cookies iced to look like pumpkins and black cats. The clock on the wall read eleven forty-five, and all around her were couples in Halloween costumes, dancing to a sweet, familiar song—"Earth Angel."

Slowly, Phoebe seemed to move through the crowd, as if searching for something or someone. Then she saw them: a tall, handsome pirate and a princess in a sparkling tiara and a long, pale lavender dress. Betty Warren and Ronald Galvez.

Betty and Ronald didn't look like a couple about to break up. They were totally in love, if the expressions on their faces were any indication. Phoebe drifted a little closer. Close enough to hear Ronald's voice.

"Let's get out of here," she heard him murmur.

Betty nodded. Ronald took her hand and led her off the dance floor toward a back room.

Without warning, Phoebe's eyesight seemed to blur. For a moment, she thought her vision was ending and she was returning to the present. When Phoebe could see clearly again, she was still at the party. She didn't see Betty and Ronald anymore. But she saw someone else: Charlotte in her long pink dress.

Phoebe watched as Charlotte plowed her way through the dance floor, her face filled with determination. She, too, headed off in the direction of the back room. Then she vanished from sight.

Moments later the screaming started.

As Phoebe watched in horror, Betty staggered back out onto the dance floor, the front of her dress covered with blood.

"Ronald," she gasped out. "Ronald—save—Charlotte!" Then she collapsed. Phoebe's eyesight blurred once more.

This time when it cleared, she was in the back room, the scene of the actual murders. Charlotte Logan lay on the floor. Bright red blood gushed from wounds on her chest and stomach.

Above her stood Ronald Galvez—holding a bloody knife.

Phoebe's eyesight went to total black. When she came to herself again, she was standing in her own hall, wrapped in Piper's arms.

"Phoebs, what is it?" Piper whispered. "I've never seen you react like that to a vision. You were shaking, crying out."

"I saw it," Phoebe whispered. "I saw the scene of the murders, Piper."

"Did you see who did it?" Piper asked as she

led Phoebe toward the kitchen. She settled her into one of the chairs at the kitchen table, then put the kettle on.

Phoebe shook her head in answer to Piper's question. "I don't think so. I saw what everybody *thinks* happened, but I don't think it's the whole story. I'm sure there's more. I wish I could talk to Charlotte's ghost again and ask her about the masked guy. I mean, why is he haunting me?"

Piper got out mugs and plunked tea bags into them. "Do you want to try to summon Charlotte together?"

Phoebe shook her head again. "I've been trying. There's not even a glimmer of response. It's as though she's elsewhere."

"Well, then," Piper said, her tone sensible, "tomorrow night we'll just have to find out what really happened."

Phoebe squeezed her sister's hand. "I'm glad you're back."

"Trust me, I am, too," Piper said. The kettle whistled, and she went over to the stove and poured hot water into the cups. "Now all we have to do is get Prue back to normal."

"It'll be good to have backup tomorrow night," Phoebe agreed. "Just in case something goes wrong."

"Like what?" Piper asked.

"I don't know," Phoebe answered.

Piper raised one dark eyebrow. "Something's bugging you."

Phoebe nodded and took a sip of tea. "In my vision . . . one of the girls who was murdered . . . her costume was identical to the one I rented this afternoon."

"Prue, have you listened to a single word I said? You can't go out with Dylan! It's too dangerous. *He's a warlock!"*

Prue slammed her hairbrush down onto the bathroom counter. "No, I haven't been listening to you, Piper," she said. "I didn't listen at breakfast. I didn't listen at lunch. And I'm certainly not going to start listening now."

"But—" Piper said. Prue cut her off, stalking out of the bathroom and into her room to finish dressing for her Sunday evening date.

The truth was, Piper was starting to feel pretty desperate. She'd tried all day to get Prue to see the truth about Dylan. She might as well have been talking to a brick wall for all the effect her words had. Prue steadfastly refused to believe her—refused even to listen!

Piper felt a bit of hope as she saw Phoebe coming up the stairs, holding a plastic clothing bag. "How'd it go?" she asked.

"Good and bad," Phoebe replied. "I managed to snag costumes for you and Prue, but there wasn't anything left that fit me. Last minute, Halloween Day and all. So I'm stuck with the lavender dress."

"What did you get me?" Piper asked, willing

to temporarily distract herself from the Prue crisis.

Phoebe held up a white cat suit, complete with fake emerald collar. "I know it's a little tacky, but—"

"It's fine," Piper said. "What about Prue?"

Phoebe grinned. "She's going to kill me." Phoebe held up a black witch's costume, complete with a pointy black hat.

Piper laughed. "Well, they say being obvious is the best disguise."

"Forget it, both of you." Prue stepped out of her room, dressed in an ice blue sheath that perfectly matched the color of her eyes. "I'm not going anywhere tonight except on my date with Dylan."

Piper sighed. "Does the word *warlock* mean anything to you?"

"I know what you're trying to do," Prue said. "You bombed with Dylan, so now you're trying to get me to back off. Well, it won't work, Piper. You had your chance. My date with Dylan starts in twenty minutes. I'm going, so stop trying to change my mind. You can't."

"What about me?" Phoebe spoke up. "I need you to go to the Halloween party with me tonight. It's important. If I don't have you and Piper backing me up, people—like me—could get killed."

Prue ignored that totally. "I mean it, Piper," she went on. "Dylan's mine now. You'll just have to deal with it."

At the mention of Dylan's name, Piper felt a blaze of white heat roar through her. Dylan wasn't Prue's, and she would prove it to her! She'd—Piper took a deep, deliberate breath and fought back the crazy whirl of feelings.

They weren't really *her* feelings anyway. She knew that now. They were the result of Dylan's spell, the powder he'd given her.

It was unfortunate that she'd been unable to convince Prue of Dylan's true nature. She could only hope her failure wasn't also fatal. Piper could think of only one reason for Dylan's actions. He wanted the powers of the Charmed Ones.

"Don't wait up for me," Prue called as she waltzed down the stairs and toward the front door.

Phoebe glanced nervously at Piper. "Should we try the measure of last resort?"

"We don't have a choice," Piper replied in a grim tone.

She clasped Phoebe's hand in hers, and quietly, in a whisper, they began to chant,

"Moon over water, change the tides of the sea,
Moon over land, work the change I decree.
For one who is held in a warlock's spell—"

"You'd actually use your powers against me?" Prue's outraged shout broke through their chant. "Fine, then all's fair—"

With that she lifted her hands, and Piper and

Phoebe found themselves flying backward up the stairway and through the open attic door.

Piper landed hard on the floor with a thump. Phoebe, she noticed, came down a little more gently on the old sofa. Then the attic door slammed shut so hard that the windows rattled.

"Wow," Phoebe said, blinking. "I've never been on the receiving end of one of Prue's telekinetic blasts before. That was impressive."

"Tell me about it," Piper said, rubbing her backside.

Phoebe got to her feet, walked over to the attic door, and tried the knob.

"Locked?" Piper guessed.

Phoebe nodded.

Piper went to the attic window and stared down at the street, watching Prue's car pull away from the curb.

Piper felt a wave of despair wash over her. "Be careful, Prue," she whispered. "Please, please be careful."

CHAPTER 11

Prue barely had time to look around the luxurious hotel suite before Dylan pulled her into his arms. "You are incredible," he murmured.

She could smell the warm, musky scent of his cologne as his lips met hers in a passionate kiss. Prue was wildly, deliriously happy. If only Piper could see her now, this moment would be perfect.

Dylan's lips moved to the side of her neck, then he stopped and slipped his finger under the necklace she wore. "Take this off," he said in a husky voice. "It's in my way."

Prue pulled away from him, wanting to slow things down and tease him just a little. "Okay," she agreed. "I'll be right back."

Before he could protest she disappeared into the bathroom. She'd take off the necklace and her heels, and undo her French braid. When she went back out into the suite's living room, Dylan would know she was ready for serious romance.

She slipped off the necklace, then began to unbraid her hair, but her reflection stopped her. Her face looked different somehow. There was something cold and calculating in her eyes. When had that become part of her?

She stood perfectly still for a moment, trying to figure it out. That look had been there for a while, she realized. Ever since she met Dylan. Could falling for a guy really change you in such a noticeable way? she wondered.

She leaned forward and peered into the mirror. Now that she had a door between herself and Dylan, she felt herself calming down. She realized that she didn't feel quite so crazed about him.

It wasn't that Dylan had changed. He was as handsome as ever. But looks aren't everything, Prue reminded herself. In fact, they aren't much more than genetic luck.

Yes, but Dylan's got more than looks, Prue thought. He's talented and funny and charming, and yet something about him had set the alarm bells ringing in the back of her brain.

Maybe it was because instead of taking her to dinner first, as they'd discussed, he'd persuaded her to go straight back to his hotel with him. He said it was to see the view, but it was clear from the moment they reached the suite that the view was not what Dylan was interested in.

Is he moving too fast? Prue asked herself. *Isn't this exactly what I wanted—to be alone with Dylan?*

Now that she was, Prue found herself wishing she were someplace else—someplace with a lot of other people around.

"What's the matter with me?" she asked her reflection.

But her reflection held no answers, only a chill look in her eyes that Prue found disturbing. Rather than keep staring at herself, Prue went back out into the living room of the suite.

"There you are, Prue," Dylan said. He was carrying a drink in each hand. "I've taken the liberty of ordering up some room service," he went on as he handed Prue her drink. "That way, we won't have to be disturbed for the rest of the evening. I can have you all to myself."

He took a step closer. Involuntarily, Prue took a step back.

Dylan's eyes narrowed. "Don't do that!" he snapped.

Prue felt a wave of shock pass through her body. Did he actually think he could order her around? Tell her how to behave?

She took another step back and set her drink down on the marble-topped table. "I'm sorry, Dylan," she said. "But I think—I think I've made a mistake."

To her astonishment, Dylan threw back his head and laughed.

"You have, Prue," he answered. "You have made a mistake. One that's going to prove fatal, I'm afraid. But don't worry." In the blink of an eye, Dylan was standing behind her. "I'll make it quick."

Desperately, Prue stumbled away as he laughed again. Oh, no! Dylan was a warlock, just as Piper had said!

"I'll bet Piper tried to warn you, didn't she?" Dylan taunted her. "But you didn't listen, did you, Prue?"

Prue tried to answer, to tell him that she was through listening to him, but the words stuck in her throat.

"I wouldn't worry about it," Dylan went on, his tone casual. "It's not your fault, you see. It's all part of my plan. I knew the only way I could get the powers of the Charmed Ones for myself was to make sure you couldn't work together. Divide and conquer. It's the oldest trick in the book."

And she'd fallen for it, Prue thought. Like a greedy fish, she'd swallowed the hook. Now, she was going to pay for it—with her powers and her life.

"I won't let you hurt my sisters," she said, determined to put on as brave a front as she could.

Dylan only laughed again. "You can't stop

me," he said. "You're all alone now, Prue. Neither of your precious sisters is going to come to save you, especially not Piper. I made quite sure of that. Watching you girls fight over me was really very entertaining."

"Bet we have the last laugh," a new voice said.

Prue's heart gave a leap. She'd know that voice anywhere! Startled, Dylan spun around.

"Piper?" he asked, staring at an oversize white cat.

Piper removed the costume's white mask. "Pleased to see me?" she asked.

"What are you doing here?" he gasped.

"Nothing you're going to like," Piper assured him.

With a roar of outrage, Dylan launched a bolt of power straight at Piper. Quickly, she raised her hands. The bolt froze halfway across the room.

Prue dashed toward her sister. "Piper, I'm so sorry!" she said.

"Do the mushy stuff later," Phoebe advised as she stepped into view. She was dressed as a fairy princess in a pale lavender gown, which Prue was sure would make sense, sooner or later.

"Meanwhile," Phoebe went on, "I suggest you get ready to deflect."

Prue grinned. She was really going to enjoy this. Dylan had done something she'd thought was impossible. He'd come between the

Halliwell sisters. Now he was going to pay the price for that.

Prue positioned herself in front of her sisters. "Ready whenever you are," she said.

Piper unfroze time. The deadly bolt hurtled straight toward Prue. At the very last moment, Prue extended her arms, palms up, and sent it hurtling back.

Dylan gave a roar of pain and outrage as his own weapon struck him, full in the chest. For one brief moment, Prue's nostrils were filled with the smell of ozone, a hot electrical scent. The warlock vanished in a puff of smoke.

"That was easy," Prue said with a sigh of relief. "Thanks to you two, that is."

Piper shook her head. "He was so full of himself," she said. "So sure of his own powers. But in the end, he never had a chance against the Power of Three."

"So, that was Mr. Right, huh?" Phoebe chimed in. "Next time you guys diss *my* choice in men, I'm definitely going to remember this."

Prue turned to her sisters and was instantly enfolded in a three-way hug. Now that Dylan was destroyed, his power over Prue and Piper was, too.

"Piper, I'm so sorry," Prue said.

"I'm sorry, too, Prue," Piper confessed. "Let's just hope it never happens again."

"It never will if I have anything to do or say about it!" Prue promised.

Phoebe headed for the door. "Come on, you two. We've got a Halloween party to get to first—not to mention a mystery to solve and a murderer to catch."

"Wow!" Prue exclaimed, as the sisters left Dylan's apartment. "I really have been out of it, haven't I?"

"Don't worry," Piper said, giving her shoulders a squeeze. "You drive. Phoebe and I will fill you in. Then we'll give you your costume."

"Whatever you say," Prue said. "Just tell me where I'm going."

"To my campus," Phoebe said. "Specifically, to Thayer Hall, where, in 1958, this whole thing began. . . ."

"Wow," Phoebe murmured forty minutes later as she and her sisters entered Thayer Hall. "This is absolutely incredible."

Though Phoebe had helped put up some of the decorations, she was totally unprepared for the effect that had been created. Not only had last night's decorating party come close to the original, it was almost a perfect replica of what she'd seen in her vision.

Too perfect, she thought, as a shiver of dread tiptoed down her spine.

"Well, Ms. Halliwell, I'm sure this will help you with your extra-credit assignment."

Phoebe yanked herself from her troubled reverie and turned toward the familiar voice. It was Professor Hagin. Phoebe almost choked when she saw the costume he had chosen.

Professor Hagin was dressed as a box of chalk.

"Excellent verisimilitude," the professor went on.

"That means it looks right," Prue whispered helpfully.

I knew that, Phoebe thought. She pinched her sister's arm.

"My research tells me this is precisely what the room looked like on that night in 1958. Plus you and Mr. Weir have both chosen the appropriate costumes, I see. You are dressed as Betty, and Mr. Weir as Ronald. It is a really exceptional historical re-creation. I commend you both."

He turned to congratulate Stan on the decor, leaving Phoebe in a state of complete shock, and dread.

"What's wrong, Phoebs?" Piper asked. "You look weird."

Phoebe shook her head. "I knew my costume was like Betty's," she said, "but not that Brett was going to come in Ronald's costume! That is *too* strange."

Prue looked puzzled. "Who's Brett?"

"He is," Phoebe snapped, pointing to the pirate who was standing by the punch bowl.

Phoebe stormed up to him. "Did you do this on purpose?" she demanded. "Did you know that on the night of the murders Ronald Galvez came to the party as a pirate?"

"Not until Hagin just told me," Brett answered, his tone surly. Phoebe had seen Brett in class, of course, but she hadn't really spoken to him since their encounter in the study hall. They hadn't talked about Wendy Chang at all.

"I left getting my costume until kind of late, and this was all the costume shop had left that fit me," Brett explained. "I don't see what you're getting so upset about, Phoebe. Having Hagin see us in these costumes may really clinch our grade." His eyes narrowed. "How come you picked yours?"

"I'm not sure," Phoebe admitted. "I guess it just seemed right at the time. Then when I tried to exchange it for something else, I ran into the same trouble you did."

Without warning, Phoebe felt another shiver slither through her. This was just the kind of thing she was worried about. Unpredictable things. Things she wouldn't be able to see coming and wouldn't be able to control.

She'd agreed to help Charlotte, to come to the party to witness what had happened in 1958, not to play a role in the actual events themselves.

The simple truth was that knowing she was dressed as Betty Warren was giving Phoebe the creeps, big time.

"Hi, I'm Brett Weir," Phoebe heard Brett say. She came out of her thoughts in time to see him smiling his big-toothed smile and offering to shake hands with Piper.

Oh no you don't! Phoebe thought. The last thing she needed was more guy trouble.

"These are my sisters," she said, taking Prue and Piper each by an arm. "Will you excuse us, please, Brett?" Death-gripping their elbows, Phoebe dragged her sisters away.

"Hey, Phoebe, take it easy," Piper protested. "I may actually need that arm someday."

"Sorry," Phoebe said, as she released her tight grip. "I just didn't want us to spend any more time with that jerk than we had to. We have more important things to concentrate on."

Prue was looking back over her shoulder at Brett. "Is that your project partner?"

Phoebe nodded.

"Phoebs, we should talk about your taste in men," Prue said seriously. Piper snickered.

Phoebe rolled her eyes. "Oh, come on you guys. I get at least six months of comment-free dating after what I just had to put up with about you guys and Dylan."

Prue reached over and gave her a swift hug. "Just teasing," she and Piper said.

Phoebe made a face.

"So, what's the plan?" Piper inquired.

"Well," Phoebe answered, "you guys have never been here before, right? So, I'm thinking maybe you should mingle a little. Get the lay of the land. That way, if something unexpected happens, we'll all know how to get out, or find some help, fast."

"Sounds good," Piper said. "Maybe we should meet by the punch table in—what?"

"How about fifteen minutes?" Prue suggested. "It shouldn't take all that long to get the layout straight. And somehow I have this feeling we should stick together as much as we can."

"I hear that!" Phoebe said. "Okay, see you in fifteen." She watched as her sisters moved off through the costumed crowd.

"Whoa, great costume," a guy in an octopus getup commented as he tried to put as many of his rubber arms as he could around Prue. "Gonna put a spell on me, wicked witch?"

Prue took the two rubber arms he'd managed to make contact with and tied them in a knot. "Not even necessary," she told him.

Phoebe turned to survey the room. "Great Balls of Fire" was playing, and the dance floor was filling up. She glanced at the clock. It was eight P.M. The night was still young. Then in the corner of the room she caught a glimpse of a young woman in a bloodied pink gown—Charlotte!

The ghost drifted unnoticed through the crowd until she stood in front of Phoebe. "Now the past must repeat itself," she said. "You must re-create it by altering time."

Phoebe blinked. "What do you mean?"

"You have powers," Charlotte said. "To know the truth, you must use them to go inside the night that was."

Phoebe thought quickly. Her sisters were just

across the room. She was perfectly safe. So would it be so terrible to do a little time-altering spell?

"Okay," she agreed. She thought back to a spell she'd seen in *The Book of Shadows*, then murmured, "Curtain of Time and all that's concealed, open into the past and its secrets reveal. Past into present, show yourself to me. As I will it, so must it be."

Phoebe felt an odd buzz of energy go through her. She glanced up at the clock in astonishment. The hands were moving swiftly around until they stopped at 11:45—the time she'd seen in her last vision of the party. Charlotte stood in front of her, smiling. Her dress was no longer covered with blood. And yet Phoebe could see Prue and Piper across the room in their hokey costumes. The spell had worked. The past was repeating itself—but inside the present.

Then Phoebe saw someone else from the present. Marjorie Yarnell was standing just inside the door. The older woman's face was the color of Professor Hagin's chalk costume, a dull, unnatural white. As Phoebe watched, Marjorie swayed, clutching at the doorjamb as if to keep herself from falling. Phoebe hurried toward her.

"Marjorie!" she exclaimed. "Are you all right?"

As Marjorie's fingers closed on her arm, Phoebe felt an icy chill sweep over her entire body, the other woman's terror was so strong. The only other time Phoebe felt that kind of connection was when she was having a vision.

"Phoebe," Marjorie gasped out. "You've got to stop this—cancel the party. Do it *now,* before something goes wrong. I have a bad feeling—such a bad feeling—"

"It's all right," Phoebe said soothingly, though she was far from believing her own words. "Just try to calm down. Come on over here. There's a quiet place where you can sit down."

Quickly, Phoebe led Marjorie to a small side room where she knew there was a couch. Only the main downstairs room of Thayer Hall had been decorated for the Halloween party. All the other rooms had been left as they were.

Phoebe urged Marjorie down onto the couch, then sat down beside her.

Marjorie seized both Phoebe's hands in her own. "I know you think I'm a crazy old woman," she said. "But you've got to listen to me, Phoebe. This party can't go on. It's got to stop—now. The past—I'm so afraid the past is going to repeat itself!"

That's because it will, Phoebe thought with a feeling of dread, but she didn't dare voice that aloud. The last thing she needed to do was make Marjorie even more hysterical.

The older woman began to sob. Phoebe held her hand, feeling helpless. She really wished she *could* call the whole party off, just send everyone home now before there was even a risk of anyone getting killed. But that wouldn't help Charlotte or the other two ghosts who continued to haunt Thayer Hall, and she had promised to help them.

"Listen to me, Marjorie," Phoebe said, trying to keep her voice calm. "I can't stop this party. There are too many people out there having a good time. But I don't think you're crazy, and I understand you being scared. I'm going to get someone to take you home."

"No!" Marjorie protested. "My safety is not the point. Someone else is going to get hurt."

"Sshhh," Phoebe said, getting to her feet. "Just wait right there. I'll be back in a minute."

Phoebe ran back out to the dance floor, where a song was playing. She'd just had a brilliant idea, one that would get Marjorie home and also ease her own mind about Brett in his pirate costume.

Phoebe looked around for Brett but couldn't see him anywhere. Nor could she see Prue and Piper. Right at the moment Phoebe really needed to call in the reinforcements, the reinforcements were gone.

"Phoebe! There you are. Why'd you run off like that?"

Phoebe felt herself grabbed and turned as the song ended. A moment later she was enveloped in Brett's arms.

"Brett," Phoebe said as another song began. "I was looking for you. I need your help."

Brett grinned down at her. "Name it."

"Marjorie Yarnell is here, and she's seriously upset. I need you to take her home."

"Later." Brett laughed and tightened his arms around her. Phoebe began to wonder if somebody had spiked the punch. She struggled, but Brett just laughed and held her closer.

"It's really nice that you're so concerned about Marjorie," he said, beginning to dance with her. "But we can't break things up yet. They're playing our song."

With a shock, Phoebe realized she recognized the song she and Brett were dancing to. It was "Earth Angel," the same one she'd heard in her vision of Betty and Ronald. The one that had been playing right before the murders.

Marjorie is right. The past is repeating itself, Phoebe thought. *And I've been cast in the role of Betty Warren.*

"Brett, please," she said. "You've got to listen."

"Oh, no," Brett Weir said. "I'll listen later. I'm not letting you get away from me this time."

He held her closer, swaying in time to the music. Phoebe could feel a sense of panic envelop her like a fog.

What year was she really in? Was she still Phoebe Halliwell, looking for the masked guy? Or was she Betty Warren in 1958?

Phoebe craned her neck, searching the crowded dance floor for Prue and Piper—and for the guy in the wolf mask. All she could see were the other partygoers, all in costume. She felt exactly as if she was standing inside her own vision of the day before, the one that had ended in murder.

Somewhere in this room, there's a killer, Phoebe thought. *But where? And who?*

And how, when Betty Warren had ended up dead, was Phoebe Halliwell ever going to get out of this alive?

CHAPTER 12

The instant "Earth Angel" was over, Phoebe went into action, finally managing to pry herself out of Brett's arms.

"Marjorie is sitting in the next room having a nervous breakdown," she reminded him. "You've got to help out and take her home."

Brett's expression turned surly. "Why are you so determined to ruin a good party?" he asked. "I'm sure Marjorie is fine."

"She's not," Phoebe insisted. "She's absolutely terrified."

"If you're going to be so hyper about it, all right," Brett finally agreed. "Let's get out of here."

Phoebe felt her blood run cold at his words. Wasn't that exactly what Ronald had said to Betty in Phoebe's vision?

"I need to find my coat," Brett said. He grabbed Phoebe's hand and pulled her toward one of the back rooms.

No! I can't let this happen! Phoebe thought.

Brett had spoken the same words that Ronald had in 1958. Now he was taking her in the same direction Ronald had taken Betty that fateful night.

"Brett," Phoebe gasped, "we're going the wrong way." She tried to pull back, but Brett plowed on ahead. "Brett!" Phoebe said again. She could hear the panic in her own voice. She tried to wrench free.

"What is your problem?" Brett barked, stopping abruptly and shaking Phoebe by the arm. "All I want to do is get my jacket. Is that too much to ask? I'm doing you a favor, Phoebe. So you might just consider backing off."

"I'm sorry," Phoebe apologized. "I guess I'm just a little keyed up."

Brett continued making his way toward one of the back rooms where coats were being stored.

This is all right. It's going to be all right, Phoebe repeated over and over to herself as she followed.

The fact that they were going to a back room, *the* back room where the murders had occurred, was just an unlucky coincidence. It didn't mean the past was already repeating itself.

"I'll just be a minute," Brett said.

He vanished into the back room and began to rummage among the coats. Phoebe felt her hopes sink as she saw the state of the room. Coats had been thrown every which way, so many Phoebe could hardly see the floor. Who knew how long it was going to take Brett to locate his coat in this mess? What if the masked man showed up while Brett was searching?

Quickly, Phoebe grabbed one of the folding chairs that lined the edge of the dance floor and stepped inside the coat room with Brett. She shut the door, then wedged the chair under the doorknob.

"Now what are you doing?" Brett asked irritably.

"Making sure nobody else can get in," Phoebe replied. "You may not be worried, but I'm not taking any chances."

"Whatever," Brett said as he resumed his search.

He thinks I've completely lost it, Phoebe thought. Well, maybe she had. Still, she'd rather be safe than sorry.

Without warning the chair began to vibrate, then shake from side to side.

Someone's trying to get in! Phoebe thought.

Wham! The chair shot from its position and flew through the air. It struck Brett in the head, hard. He went down like a stone, knocked unconscious. The door of the back room crashed back against the wall.

In the open doorway stood a girl in a pink party dress.

The ghost of Charlotte Logan.

She raised a knife, high. Its long, wicked blade glinted in the harsh overhead light of the coatroom.

"Betty Warren!" Charlotte cried. "For nearly half a century, I've waited for this moment. For the chance to kill you again. And again. *And again!*"

With a scream of hatred, she rushed toward Phoebe, plunging the knife down.

Phoebe dodged quickly, but she could hear the knife whistle through the air.

"I'm not Betty," she gasped. "I'm Phoebe Halliwell. I'm here to help you. Don't you remember, Charlotte?"

Charlotte Logan began to laugh, uncontrollably. "Oh, yes, I remember you, Betty," she said. "I remember how much you always wanted to help. Help poor Charlotte, who wasn't pretty enough, who was too shy to get a date on her own.

"You could have had any boy you wanted!" she screamed as she swung the knife again. "Why did you have to take the only boy I ever loved?"

So that's it! Phoebe thought.

Marjorie Yarnell had been right. The murders *had* been caused by jealousy. But Charlotte hadn't been jealous of Ronald. She'd been jealous of Betty. The two best friends had fallen in love with the same guy. It was a mistake that had cost Betty Warren her life.

"I'll never forgive you. Never," Charlotte declared as she moved toward Phoebe, swinging the knife in front of her. "I wanted to kill you for taking him from me. I couldn't rest for thinking about it. I've wanted to do it, again and again."

With every step forward Charlotte took, Phoebe faltered back a step. How long until she reached the wall? How long before Charlotte had her cornered? How long until Phoebe felt the gleaming blade of the knife pierce her flesh?

"Wait a minute," Phoebe said, desperately stalling for time. "What about the masked man?"

"I made him up," Charlotte replied. "You wanted another suspect, so I gave you one because I needed your help."

"No," Phoebe said, inching backward. "I saw him. I saw his ghost. He wore a wolf mask that covered his head."

Charlotte hesitated a moment, then began to laugh. "That's rich," she said. "You saw Ronald. When he first showed up at the party, he wore a wolf mask to fool Betty. He only kept it on for a minute, then he took it off."

Phoebe was thoroughly confused. "Then why would his ghost appear to me that way?"

"Probably because he was trying to scare you off," Charlotte said. "You first summoned a spirit who would take you inside. And I was the only one of us who was willing to do that."

"You mean, you were the only one who *wanted* to do that," Phoebe said, realizing exactly what the words of the spell had meant. "You wanted to take me inside as Betty, so that you could kill her again. Ronald tried to protect me from you."

"Very good." Charlotte's voice was mocking. "You're not particularly quick, but you do manage to get it in the end." She raised the knife higher and floated closer and closer to Phoebe.

Phoebe edged back, her eyes on the blade.

In horror, Phoebe felt her foot slip as she stepped on one of the coats. She tumbled back.

"Now!" Charlotte cried, springing forward. "Now, once more, I will have my revenge!"

"I don't think so," a new voice said.

Charlotte spun toward the sound, knife still raised high. A moment later, it shot from her hands. It landed against the far wall with a clatter. The ghost darted toward it, and was thrown in the opposite direction.

"Stay away from my sister!" Prue cried.

"No!" Charlotte shrieked. "I've got to kill her. I must kill Betty."

She reached for Phoebe with her bare hands.

"*Charlotte!*" cried a voice Phoebe recognized.

No, it can't be! she thought.

Charlotte paused. Her fingers still reached for Phoebe, but now there was a look of confusion on her face. Her head swiveled toward the doorway.

"Betty?" she gasped. "But that can't be. You're dead. You died that night in 1958. I know you did. I killed you myself!"

"No, you didn't, Charlotte," Marjorie Yarnell said. "I'm standing right here."

Phoebe could literally feel her head begin to swim. The answer to the mystery had been beside her the whole time, and she'd never recognized it. Marjorie Yarnell was Betty.

"But how—" Phoebe gasped.

"I was seriously wounded the night of the party," Marjorie explained. "But, fortunately, I was taken to a hospital in time. My family was powerful enough to keep my identity a secret. Physically, I recovered and moved far away. I even changed my name so that no one would associate me with the events of that terrible night. I became Marjorie Yarnell.

"But even though my body healed, my mind was always tormented. The trauma of the attack erased most of its details. Whenever I tried to look back, I couldn't seem to do it. The truth was simply too terrible to contemplate. Either I'd been attacked by the man I loved, or by my very best friend."

Poor Marjorie! Phoebe thought, rising to her feet. How she must have suffered all these years—unsure of who to believe, which memories to trust. Knowing that one of the two people she'd loved most in the world had been guilty of the worst kind of betrayal.

"Marjorie, I'm so sorry," Phoebe said.

"Don't be, Phoebe," Marjorie Yarnell answered. "I knew I would have to come back here sooner or later, to put the demons from my past to rest. Now I've done it. I know the truth. I remember everything. Being here, in this room, on this night, has brought it all back."

Marjorie pointed a finger at the ghost of Charlotte.

"It was you!" Marjorie said. "You knew Ronald and I were going to elope that night. You knew because I'd told you all our plans. You were always jealous of Ronald and me. You didn't want our love to have a happy ending."

"What about me?" the ghost of Charlotte Logan demanded. "Didn't I deserve a happy ending? You could have had any boy you wanted. But you chose the boy I loved."

"I didn't know," Marjorie whispered. "You never told me."

Charlotte gave a bitter laugh. "That's right," she said. "I never told you. Instead, I listened, day after day, while you told me all your plans. When you said you and Ronald were going to elope, I had to stop you. I'd given up hoping Ronald would love me by that time, but I wasn't about to let you have him."

"If you couldn't have him, nobody could, is that it?" Marjorie asked.

I'll never hear that cliché the same way again, Phoebe thought.

"That's right!" Charlotte said, her tone triumphant. "After you staggered out of here, Ronald and I struggled for the knife. In the struggle, I stabbed myself, then handed the knife to him. He was still holding it when the others burst into the room. That's the way they found him."

"You killed him!" Marjorie cried out. "You made certain Ronald would be blamed for what you did. You never loved him. You only loved yourself. And to think that, for all these years, I thought you were my friend."

"I was never your friend," Charlotte told her. "You were gullible—just as stupid as Phoebe is. I'm the only one who was smart—the only one who was clever. Clever enough to get away with murder for all these years."

"I don't know about you guys, but I think I've heard enough," Piper's voice cut in.

"Shall we waste her for you?" Prue asked Marjorie. "We can do that, you know."

"Really? Then please," Marjorie Yarnell said. "I think that would be best. She's hurt enough people and ruined enough lives. It's time she was stopped."

"Okay, let's do it," Phoebe said.

Quickly, she and her sisters joined hands. Prue began an incantation that would banish forever a ghost bent on evil. Phoebe and Piper picked up the chant.

"No!" the ghost of Charlotte cried out, rushing forward. "You can't!"

"Actually, we can," Phoebe said.

Charlotte's ghost exploded into a shower of hot sparks. For a moment, the room was filled with a tumble of bright light. Then there was nothing but ash.

"I think that takes care of that!" Phoebe said.

"Whew! I'm glad none of these coats are mine," Piper said.

"I'm not going to ask why or how you girls can do that," Marjorie Yarnell said. "I'm just grateful that you can. I hope, wherever she is, that Charlotte is at peace now. I truly never meant to hurt her. I thought I was her friend."

"Betty."

In the center of the room, a wavery figure was appearing.

"Oh, wow," Piper said.

"Ronald?" Marjorie answered, her voice choked with tears. "Ronald, is that you?"

The figure grew solid. Now Phoebe could see it was a young man. She recognized him at once from her visions.

Ronald Galvez was dressed in his pirate costume, a gold earring glinting in one ear. He was as devastatingly handsome now as he'd been in his yearbook photos.

"Yes, Betty, it's me," Ronald said gently. "It's time for me to go now, too. But I had to see you again."

Marjorie stumbled forward, toward the ghost of the true love she'd lost so long ago.

"Ronald, I'm sorry," she said. "Sorry I ever doubted you, believed you could ever be anything other than innocent."

"It's all right," Ronald Galvez said. "It was all

part of Charlotte's evil. Not only did she drive us apart, she made you doubt my feelings. But I never stopped loving you, not in the instant of my death, or all the years since."

Phoebe could see tears streaming down Marjorie's cheeks. She felt her own eyes fill.

"I owe your friend Phoebe an apology," Ronald said. He turned to Phoebe. "I'm sorry for trying to frighten you, but since you didn't summon me, it was the only way I could warn you off. I couldn't let Charlotte kill a second time."

Phoebe remembered the mysterious energy that pushed her out of the way of the crashing bookshelves. "Were you the one who pushed me in the library?"

"Guilty," Ronald admitted with a grin.

I can see why Betty fell so hard for him, Phoebe thought. For all of his bad boy looks, it was plain that Ronald had a good heart.

"Believe me, I appreciated that," Phoebe said. "So no hard feelings."

"I'm glad," Ronald Galvez said. "And in the end, I'm glad I couldn't stop you. You and your sisters have made it possible for me to be at peace. After all these years, you've helped me clear my name. Now that Betty—Marjorie—knows the truth, I can finally rest."

"Ronald," Marjorie whispered. "I'm not sure I can bear to lose you all over again."

The ghost of Ronald Galvez lifted a hand. He brushed it lightly, not quite touching, over

Marjorie's cheek. "But you never really lost me," he said. "I've been watching over you for all these years. Now that Charlotte's evil has been destroyed, not even death can stand between us. I know we'll be together in the end."

As Phoebe watched, a soft white light began to glow around Ronald's figure.

"Whenever you get here, I'll be waiting, Betty," he said.

The light flared, growing so bright Phoebe had to raise a hand to shield her eyes. When she lowered it, Ronald Galvez was gone. Marjorie stood alone in the center of the room, her head bowed, her hands clasped.

Silently, Phoebe put an arm around her and led her from the room that had seen so many of her dreams come to an end. Prue and Piper followed. Prue shut the door behind them.

In the hallway, Marjorie stopped. "Thank you," she said. "All of you. I don't think I'll be haunted by the past any longer."

Phoebe gave Marjorie a hug. "I hope you won't," she said. "But if you are, you know where to come."

A soft smile crossed Marjorie's features. "Yes, I guess I do," she said. "I knew you were special the moment I saw you," she told Phoebe. "I just didn't have any idea *how* special. Now, if you girls will excuse me—"

Before Phoebe and her sisters could protest, Marjorie moved off toward the dance floor and disappeared into the crowd. With a sense of shock, Phoebe realized there was still a party going on all around her.

"Oh, my God. I think I left Brett in the coat room!" she said. Quickly, she peeked into the room again. Brett was sitting up, rubbing his head.

"He's going to be okay," Prue said over her shoulder.

Phoebe turned as a young woman dressed as a nurse made her way through the crowd, calling Brett's name.

"Wendy has no idea how appropriate her costume is," Phoebe said with smile. "Would one of you mind telling her where she can find her boyfriend? She won't want to hear it from me."

"My pleasure," Piper said.

A few moments later Phoebe and her sisters made their way through the crowd of dancers.

"It's just such a creepy story," Phoebe heard one girl say. "I mean, imagine that girl, Charlotte, killing her best friend, then setting up her friend's boyfriend to take the blame. Serves her right that she ended up dead. I mean, is that right out of the tabloids, or what?"

"Definitely," the guy she was dancing with said.

"Did you hear that?" Phoebe asked as she and her sisters broke through the crowd and walked toward the exit. "When we destroyed Charlotte, we must have 'updated' the legend of the Halloween murders somehow. Now the story is correct."

"I'd say Ronald and Betty sort of got their happily-ever-after ending, after all," Piper said. "Ronald's been cleared, and Charlotte gets the blame."

"Excellent," Phoebe said. "Hey, wait a minute. I wonder if this is going to affect my extra-credit grade!"

"I wouldn't worry about it if I were you," Prue commented as they got into her car. "You've still got a whole semester ahead of you."

"Let's just hope the other legends aren't quite as dangerous as this one was!" Phoebe said.

As Prue started the car and drove away, Phoebe looked back at the bright lights of Thayer Hall. Her grade really didn't make that much difference to her, she thought. In her heart, Phoebe knew she'd accomplished something much more important.

"I'm hungry!" Prue announced as she turned the corner and the lights of the campus vanished. "Can I interest either of you in a quick stop for sushi?"

"I know this great new place in Pacific Heights." Phoebe smiled. "If we hurry, we'll beat the rush!"

About the Author

CAMERON DOKEY is the author of more than twenty novels including *Love Me, Love Me Not*, named as a Best Book for Teens by the New York Public Library. She lives with her husband and an assortment of cats in Seattle, Washington.

. . . A GIRL BORN
WITHOUT THE FEAR GENE

FEARLESS™

A SERIES BY
FRANCINE PASCAL

FROM POCKET PULSE
PUBLISHED BY POCKET BOOKS

3029